Excellent Intentions

Excellent Intentions

Richard Hull

With an Introduction
by Martin Edwards

Poisoned Pen Press

Originally published in 1938 by Faber & Faber
©Richard Hull 1938
Introduction Copyright © 2018 by Martin Edwards
Published by Poisoned Pen Press in association with
the British Library

First U.S. Edition 2018

10 9 8 7 6 5 4 3 2 1

Library of Congress Control Number: 2018940613

ISBN: 9781464209758   Trade Paperback
ISBN: 9781464209765   Ebook

Poisoned Pen Press
4014 N. Goldwater Blvd., #201
Scottsdale, AZ 85251
www.poisonedpenpress.com
info@poisonedpenpress.com

Printed in the United States of America

Introduction

Excellent Intentions, re-titled *Beyond Reasonable Doubt* on its first appearance in the US, is a courtroom mystery with a difference. On the dust jacket of the first edition, the publishers Faber hailed Richard Hull's flair for finding new ways to tell a tale about crime, and said that with this book "we are beginning to believe his gifts to be inexhaustible… Even for Richard Hull, this is an unusual murder story."

The reader is plunged at once into the trial of a murderer. It is soon evident that the victim—as so often in mysteries written during the Golden Age of Murder between the world wars—was thoroughly deserving of his fate. The suspects are introduced, as is the low-key but capable Inspector Fenby. What is not made clear—and this is a key puzzle to challenge the reader—is the identity of the person in the dock.

Hull was writing at a time when the notion of the "altruistic crime" held a special fascination for leading crime novelists. Agatha Christie, Anthony Berkeley, and John Dickson Carr were among those who tackled the concept in an entertaining and often thought-provoking way, and *Excellent Intentions* is an enjoyable example of this sub-genre. Reviewers who admired the novel included, improbably enough, Jorge Luis Borges, who said: "Richard Hull has written an extremely pleasant book. His prose is able, his characters convincing, his irony civilized." Yet until now, it has long been out of print.

Richard Hull's real name was Richard Henry Sampson. He was born in 1896, the youngest of five siblings, and followed his two brothers to Hildersham House, Broadstairs, and Rugby School. He was very delicate as a small boy, and recalled in later life that a bout of colitis "enforced a diet of Plasmon biscuits, Frameford jelly and water and *nothing* else whatever at any meal for over a year. The necessary self-control gave me a strength of character of a most regrettable rigour."

An unassuming man, he said in a letter about the family's history to his nephew Nic that he "was an indifferent mathematician and knew it so [left Rugby] a year earlier than had been intended. As one result I absurdly got two exhibitions to which nobody else was entitled. I never took them up as I never got to Cambridge, (which was a great loss to me and would have done me a power of good), because… when war broke out I found myself given a commission on Sept. 6th 1914, my eighteenth birthday, in Queen Victoria's Rifles. Up to then I had not liked my time in the O.T.C. [Officers' Training Corps]. In some ways I never really liked soldiering—especially drill, dress and discipline—but I liked the administrative side and I also liked being one of a side. I also developed a very strong feeling for that particular battalion which has lasted all my life.

"After a period of training, (entirely in Hyde Park in London!), I managed to get sent out to France partly by mistake to the 1st Q.V.R. in April 1915. I was convinced that if I did not get out quickly the war would be over before I got out and that would be very disgraceful to me. In fact it was illegal for anyone to go out before he was nineteen, which I was not. I found myself on my first visit to the line accidentally in command of a company, owing to casualties, and told to be ready to support an attack on hill 60. But I did not have to go."

After the war, he was articled to a firm of chartered accountants, qualifying in 1922. He claimed that he "never liked accounting and I never was a good accountant... I joined the wrong partner and then tried to set up a practice of my own. 1925 to 1935 were not my most successful or profitable years." At this point, Hull's life was transformed. Impressed by Francis Iles' cynical but superb crime novel *Malice Aforethought* (1931), he came up with a clever idea for a novel of his own. *The Murder of My Aunt* (1934) proved to be a critical and commercial triumph. Fourteen more novels followed, together with at least one short story, his last book appearing in 1953.

He wrote that he "had stayed with the Q.V.R. until December 1929 when, partly because I could not afford it, I retired but I used to keep up with them and go to camp. When war broke out again in 1939 to my surprise they wanted me back. I started the morning of Sept 1st 1939 as a civilian with no idea of being anything else and ended in uniform in command of a company having got rid of my lodging and such accountancy practice as I had. It was distinctly startling." In May 1940, his troops were ordered overseas at short notice, but it was decided that Hull was too old to go with them: "I was very upset but it was really very lucky for me. They were all taken prisoner at Calais. So I missed five years in a prisoner of war camp. I more or less demobilized myself in order to use my accountancy knowledge as a cost investigating accountant for the admiralty, the idea being to see that no one was overcharging them. There I stayed for

18 years until I decided that I could retire (in 1958). It was interesting to deal with different people in different firms and to try to solve various cost-accountancy problems but I always had an uneasy suspicion that the whole department was a waste of time."

Hull's interests often found their way into his books, and a cost investigating accountant takes a leading role in *The Unfortunate Murderer* (1941). He was keen on philately and fine wine, and both play a part in *Until She Was Dead* (1950). He spent a great deal of his time at the United Universities Club in Suffolk Street, just off Trafalgar Square, and told Nic: "I have many friends there and a satisfactory supply of enemies." *Keep it Quiet* (1935), set in a fictional gentleman's club, no doubt offered him the chance to pay off a few scores.

In 1946, he was elected to membership of the Detection Club (which had been founded by Anthony Berkeley, also known as Francis Iles), along with Christianna Brand, the barrister Cyril Hare, and the American Alice Campbell. Later, Hull became the Club Secretary, and—in common with Berkeley, Dorothy L. Sayers and others—he retained his enthusiasm for the Club's activities long after his zest for actually writing crime fiction had faded. He took a leading role in making the arrangements for the initiation of Agatha Christie as President of the Club after Sayers' death, and continued to assist Christie with her duties for several years. He died in 1973, by which time most of his books had been unavailable for many years. The British Library's decision to reissue this book and *The Murder of My Aunt* gives present day readers an opportunity to acquaint themselves with one of the most innovative of crime writers.

Martin Edwards
www.martinedwardsbooks.com

Part I
Prosecution

"May it please your lordship—members of the jury," Anstruther Blayton rose to his feet and, as was his habit, moved some papers that were near him in an unnecessary and fussy manner. At the age of fifty-two he was, he knew, comparatively young to have been selected by the Attorney-General to act as leader in a trial which was arousing a certain amount of public interest. Even though he had been known for some time as a leading K.C. on the circuit, it was his chance and he meant to make the most of it.

Fairly, of course—indeed to be anything other than scrupulously fair would *not* be to make the best of the opportunity—but with real efficiency and success.

He very definitely intended to show the world at large that though he was not exactly a new star in the legal firmament, for he was already quite well known at any rate to the Bench and Bar, he was a very bright constellation indeed. And, if the result must necessarily be the hanging of the prisoner, that was not his fault. After all a verdict of "guilty" would to his mind be right, and it was for the person who committed the murder to consider the consequences, before acting; they were no business of his.

He turned and faced squarely towards the Judge. Mr. Justice Smith had a considerable reputation as one who made up his mind and usually managed to induce the jury, whatever the case might be, to agree with him. It was rumoured that he was thinking of retiring which, in Blayton's opinion, would be a pity, for he understood that Sir Trefusis Smith was a competent Judge and competent Judges were not easy to get—naturally enough considering how much a really successful K.C., such as Blayton intended to be, could earn.

Perhaps Anstruther Blayton's reflections were too condescending and his expectations too sweeping. Certainly he was a long way so far from anything of the sort. Indeed the movements and the whole attitude of counsel for the Crown did not please his lordship. Blayton had seldom, during Sir Trefusis Smith's long service on the Bench, happened to appear before him—and never when it had been essential for him to consider what type of man counsel was. Now that he had to do so, he rather took a dislike to the fresh, almost ruddy-complexioned man of medium height who was visibly trying to impress him, for Sir Trefusis was quite capable of discerning at once the intentions of those who came into his Court. Besides the whole case annoyed him. It was, he had privately decided, to be his last case and he wanted, like Falstaff, to make a good end, but definitely without the traditional "babbling".

But the case before him, he suspected, was not going to provide such a curtain. It was, he had heard, likely to prove quite simple. There was very little doubt of the guilt of the prisoner, and he would much have preferred something more complicated in which his peculiar talents would have been displayed to advantage. However, if he was going to take a prejudice to counsel for the Crown, it might make things more interesting. Then he pulled himself together. He had no right to take prejudices and still less right to hear anything or form any opinion about the case before it came into Court. No one knew that elementary platitude that was invariably recited to juries better than himself, and usually he took the greatest care to turn the precept into practice. It was just bad luck that he had happened to hear rumours, portions of the Coroner's inquest, gossip—just the things he had always before avoided. With trained ability, he turned his mind into an impartial blank. He *would* know nothing except what was told to him in Court and he settled himself to listen, sphinx-like.

"May it please your lordship—members of the jury, on Friday, July 13th—a combination of unlucky days—Launcelot Henry Cuthbert Cargate died in a railway train between Larkingfield and Great Barwick stations on the borders of Essex and Suffolk at approximately eleven-fifty-seven in the morning. On Thursday, August 9th the accused"—with a melodramatic gesture which threatened to arouse anew Mr. Justice Smith's latent prejudice, counsel pointed to the dock and rolled out unctuously the full name of its occupant—"was arrested and charged with wilfully murdering him by administering poison to him, and it is on that charge that the accused now stands before you. It will be my duty, in conjunction with my learned friend, Mr. Knight, to present the case for the Crown, while the defence is in the hands of my learned friends, Mr. Vernon and Mr. Oliver."

Anstruther Blayton hitched his gown up on to his shoulders. He considered that he had now found what pitch of his full, mellow voice was best suited to the Court, and he thought the moment had come for a few words of wisdom to impress the jury, combined of course with a little flattery.

"Members of the jury, you will I know give your closest and most prolonged attention to this case, not only because it is of unusual complexity, not only because murder is the gravest charge known to the law, but because of the nature of the evidence on which you will be asked to decide this case."

Blayton paused, feeling that he was doing excellently. That should put the jury at their ease and let them settle down in comfort, but in his more exalted position Sir Trefusis shuffled uneasily. He had during his life listened to a good many platitudes but on the whole he considered that those which Blayton was enunciating were about as bad as any that he had ever heard. Did he really think that any of the jury would consider murder to be a trivial charge? But, the "young" man was inexperienced at this particular work. Perhaps, he thought charitably, he was nervous, although he didn't look it. He supposed that he must go on listening quietly and not run the risk of worrying him by fidgeting unduly. He let his small, aquiline nose twitch imperceptibly. It was a relief and allowed him to go on listening.

Not that Blayton was, for the moment, taking any notice of him. He was continuing to concentrate almost entirely upon the jury.

"The crime of administering poison is not one which is carried out upon the house-tops before the public gaze of all men. It is almost invariably committed in secret and the evidence with regard to it must almost of necessity be indirect, circumstantial evidence, not that of an eye-witness.

"So it is in this case. For when Launcelot Henry Cuthbert Cargate—"

"I have no wish to interrupt you, Mr. Blayton, but might we in future refer to the unfortunate gentleman who is deceased a little less accurately but more concisely? I am sure that the jury will not misunderstand you."

"Certainly, my lord. I believe that he was usually known as Henry Cargate."

"Very well, then. The jury will understand that by Henry Cargate you mean Launcelot Henry Cuthbert Cargate. Perhaps even, in practice, 'the deceased' will be a sufficient description. Go on, please, Mr. Blayton."

For a moment counsel for the prosecution did not seem to know quite what point he had reached. Then he recollected and continued, trying to forgive and forget the fact that one of his best periods had been ruined.

"For when *Henry* Cargate died in, as I have told you, a railway train, the accused was not even present. Indeed it was unusual for Mr. Cargate to take a train at all. Such journeys as he had occasion to take, he usually performed by car, and for all that the accused knew or cared he might have met his death while actually at the wheel of a motor vehicle, and possibly in circumstances which might have endangered the lives of others utterly unconnected with the deceased or those about him."

In the dock the accused moved angrily. Whatever else might or might not be true, that was a lie. A reckless and criminal disregard of innocent, third parties—certainly not! Cargate was one thing. Almost anybody might reasonably have killed him. But this red-faced, fussy, blathering man had no right to stir up prejudice in that way.

"Members of the jury, for that reason and for others, I am going to suggest to you that this was a very wicked crime and I will return to that subject again when we consider the question of motive. But for the moment let us return to the crime itself. As chance would however have it, there *was* a witness present when Henry Cargate died and your attention will later on be directed to the events that then occurred. For indeed had it not happened that a certain Mr. Hardy was looking into the window of the corridor of the train at the critical moment, coupled with, let me add, his presence of mind and the courtesy and public-spirited action, combined with acumen, of the London and North Eastern Railway, this crime might never have been detected.

"Mr. Hardy will tell you…"

Mr. Hardy indeed was burning to tell them. In fact he wanted to retail this quite exciting incident in a great deal more detail than he was likely to be permitted to do in Court. His friends, of course, would hear it in ever-growing form for years to come.

Not that he was so foolish as to regard it as the most important event in his life. On the whole that must be reserved for the building of the new oven in which for ten years past he had supplied bread to all the village of Scotney End after old Smee had decided that he was too old—at ninety-two—to bake any more. It was a very fine oven and it had added very nicely to the profits of the general shop and post-office which Hardy had already been running.

But Friday, July 13th had been an important day to him weeks before it had arrived, for on it he was to visit for the first time for many years his sister who had married and gone to live in foreign parts beyond Great Barwick. It was an expedition of considerable importance for it had been decided that it involved a journey not only to Larkingfield, itself nearly five miles away, but from there by railway. True it was only for one station, but when you are able to count on the fingers of your hands the number of times that you have done anything so adventurous as travelling by a train, it becomes a matter not to be embarked upon lightly.

He had naturally arrived at the station about half an hour too soon. You never could be sure what these railway companies might do. They did say in Scotney End that the time of the only morning train never altered, but he wasn't going to run any risks. It wasn't often that he could arrange to have a free day and, if anything went wrong, it might be another few years before he got the chance again. Accordingly he was in plenty of time to see Mr. Cargate arrive at Larkingfield Station.

He was of course perfectly well aware of who Mr. Cargate was. Nobody living in the village could fail to recognize the new owner of Scotney End Hall. Not that Hardy had many dealings with him. Mr. Cargate—it was rather a grievance of Hardy's—got everything that he possibly could down from London; even his bread was some patent stuff in tins, for Mr. Cargate suffered from a weak digestion in addition to an indifferent heart. Still, there were the members of the household to be supplied, Miss Knox Forster, his middle-aged, plain secretary, Mr. Raikes, his butler, and half a dozen others. The village had at first tried to work up a scandal about his having an unmarried secretary, but one look at Miss Knox Forster had settled that. A woman clearly capable of looking after herself and definitely more competent than attractive.

Still, Scotney End on the whole thought very little of the new owner of the hall. He was a foreigner from London, not like the old Squire, and he made no attempt to overcome the handicap. Indeed he seemed capable of thinking that the village could be improved and he was always interfering in the parish. The vicar in fact was believed strongly to resent his intrusion, but perhaps it was natural that he should dislike having as his principal parishioner one who considered his church an interesting piece of architecture, but openly professed himself an atheist. There was a rumour that Cargate wanted to pull down the vestry to see if there were not the remains of a pagan temple—Roman or some such thing—underneath.

On the whole, Hardy agreed with the vicar and the village if more for the reasons which influenced the latter. Cargate clearly did not care what happened to Scotney End. He only troubled with what happened to himself. It was all very well to mind your own business—both Scotney End and Hardy were in agreement that that was a desirable thing to do—but there was a general consensus of opinion that Cargate overdid it.

But on the morning of Friday, July 13th, the first thing which intrigued Hardy—a naturally inquisitive man—was why Cargate was going by train at all. Normally his arrivals and departures from the village were made in a large and very fast Bentley which he drove at a speed unsuited to the roads round Scotney End at least. It might be all very well when you were beyond Larkingfield and got on to the main road to Great Barwick, but not in places such as the bridge over the brook by Hurst Farm where the corner was blind and there was generally a cow in the middle of the road.

However, that was beside the point. Here was Mr. Cargate getting out of the Austin that could be hired in Larkingfield, and Hardy very properly assumed that there was something wrong with the Bentley. There was also something wrong with Mr. Cargate's temper. He was tapping his umbrella angrily on the flagstones of the platform and glancing at his watch. Then, seeing the stationmaster, he called out:

"Here, you, how much longer have I got to wait for this infernal train?"

"Due in in about two minutes, sir. We shall see her come round the corner beyond the wood any—"

"The train is already two minutes late. Can't think what's coming over railways these days. No wonder nobody ever travels by them."

Hardy had stood watching, fascinated. He had never seen Harry Benson, who as stationmaster at Larkingfield was of some local importance, talked to in such a way and even interrupted. He wondered what he would do about it. On the whole Hardy was a little disappointed. Benson only shrugged his shoulders when Cargate's back was turned. He didn't trouble to make any reply at all.

Cargate himself moved a few yards down the platform in the direction from which the train would come, apparently under the impression that that would hasten its arrival. The movement brought him quite close to Hardy so that he was able to see exactly what happened next. From his pocket Cargate took a small gold-coloured box, rather thicker than a cigarette-case, with something on the lid which sparkled—at least that is how Hardy mentally described it to himself— and, opening it, put as much of a light brown powder on to his left thumb as could be conveniently placed there. It was rather clumsily done and, in fact, a few grains fell on to the platform. Though he had never taken it, Hardy recognized from what he had been told that this must be snuff. He wanted to see what happened next and without realizing what he was doing he took a pace forward.

What happened was that he caused the porter, who was wheeling Cargate's luggage down the platform, to swerve slightly so that he just touched the left arm that was about to raise the snuff to the nose of an already irritated man. It was only the merest graze but it was sufficient to send the rest of the light brown powder on to the platform. Cargate's temper gave way at once.

"What the hell do you think you're doing? Great clumsy lout! For heaven's sake go back to looking after the pigs which are your natural companions."

"I'm sorry, sir, I'm sure, but you seemed to move in to me."

"I did *nothing* of the sort." It was perfectly true but there was no need for the withering contempt in Cargate's voice. Snuff, after all, was cheap, and if he was in urgent need of its soothing influence, he had already wasted more time in abusing the porter than it would have taken to open the box and replace what had been spilt. But Cargate never had done sensible things like that. "Stationmaster! Stationmaster!" he yelled.

"What's the matter *now*, sir?"

"I'll trouble you not to be sarcastic to me. I shall undoubtedly report this when I get to Liverpool Street. Your train is late and you pretend that it isn't; you are thoroughly impertinent and offhand in your manner yourself, and this oaf of a porter of yours runs into me and then has the cheek to tell me that I ran into him. With a heart like mine, the sudden shock might well have been very bad for me."

"If you've got a bad heart, I should calm yourself, sir. I'm sure Jim here didn't mean any harm and he'll say he's sorry. Accidents will happen, sir, even in the best regulated stations."

"Which this certainly is not."

"No, sir, but we do our best." Benson did *his* best to pour oil on the troubled waters, though even at the time he couldn't imagine why he was taking so much trouble. Still, it was a good example to the porter with whom he knew he was going to have trouble directly the eleven-fifty-six had gone.

Fortunately, before Cargate could reply, a diversion was created by a nondescript brown dog which came cheerfully bounding along the platform towards them with every sign of joyous recognition.

"Here's that dog of yours again, Jim." Benson turned at once to the porter. "How often have I told you to keep him locked up properly when there's duty to be done." He didn't like telling off Jim in front of this man Cargate, but it might change the subject. Also it would anticipate the trouble that was only too likely to be brewing up. Even with porters, offence was often the best defence.

"Well, I'm sorry, sir." Jim was unexpectedly humble. "But he's that clever, he will get out."

"Then he doesn't resemble his master," Cargate snapped, "except that he's thoroughly out of hand. I notice that neither of you can control your subordinates. I shall add that to my report."

But the dog had not yet finished creating his diversion, and now, instead of being ill-omened, it glanced aside into a more propitious course, since attracted by the smell, it put its nose down to where the powder had been spilled. Apparently it did not like it at all since after a startled sneeze, it ran away howling and rubbing its nose against the paling as if something was burning it. At that moment too the train came in, and with a less indignant "Serve you right", Cargate got in. It had amused him to watch the dog's discomfiture; nevertheless he saw no reason to tip the porter and he was fully determined to complain about the whole matter. Already in his mind he was preparing the exaggerated sentences that he would use, for Cargate was well aware of the best way of getting those to whom he took a dislike into trouble. In fact he had probably done more harm to other people than almost any other private individual in the world.

During all this time Hardy had remained in the background, an interested spectator. He could, and afterwards he frequently did, give a most vivid rendering of what occurred, but that was to make up for the fact that Mr. Justice Smith did not encourage him to tell the Court about it nearly so completely as he might. Moreover, just after the train left

Larkingfield he was still an interested spectator for he shrewdly guessed that as soon as it started, Cargate would take his deferred pinch of snuff and he wanted to watch him. Quite what he expected to see, it is difficult to imagine. Perhaps it was simply that he did not know what he would see that excited his ever active curiosity.

Luck was with him. The train was only a slow one on a branch line, but Great Barwick was just sufficiently distinguished to be allowed (grudgingly) an occasional through carriage, composed partly of first and partly of third class compartments with a corridor. Consequently Hardy was able to stand in the passage, and while keeping out of Cargate's sight, watch in the window the reflection of that gentleman once more taking out his snuffbox. Indeed afterwards Hardy was invariably to say that it was the accident of that reflection which made him look. On the whole it is probable that he would have looked anyhow, directly or indirectly, and that the reflection was just a lucky chance for him but, be that as it may, he looked and he saw.

Once more he saw "the box with the sparkling lid" appear from Cargate's pocket and the light brown powder be put on the left thumb. A lot of it there was and this time the clumsiness had gone. Hardy admired the skill with which so much was kept so carefully in place. The thumb travelled surely up to Cargate's nostril and with a powerful sniff, the brown powder disappeared. For a fifth of a second Cargate's ill-natured face seemed more satisfied. Then followed a sneeze more violent than any Hardy had ever heard in his life. As if the sneeze wanted to expel everything from his nostrils. After that a slight flush appeared over his cheeks and he fell back in the seat, the box clattering on the floor and its contents being all spilled.

Hardy was only a simple country man but he didn't like the look of it all. He was sure that Cargate was very ill and he remembered the remarks which he had just heard him making about his heart. He had only been in a railway train a few times before but he was certain that he ought to do something—in fact that he ought to do the thing that he had always been told was the one thing that normally you must never do. Before the train was out of sight of Larkingfield Station, he pulled the communication cord.

Naturally the account which Hardy gave to his friends was a longer one than he gave either at the instigation of Mr. Blayton or to Inspector Fenby. Jim's dog, for instance, in whom the Inspector did show a transient interest, was not allowed to appear in Court at all, and when it came to being cross-questioned by counsel for the accused, the interest shifted to an unexpected subject.

The defence, as Blayton had so kindly told the Court, was in the hands of Mr. Vernon, K.C., assisted by Mr. Oliver, and Hardy, as the first witness, was taken in hand by the senior counsel.

"You were," suggested Vernon in a bored voice, "when the deceased took the pinch of snuff, sitting in your compartment?"

"No, sir, I was standing in the corridor." Considering that he had said so already only a few minutes before, Hardy was rather nettled by the question.

"And looking out of the window?"

"Yes, sir, and into the window, if you see what I mean."

"I am quite able to follow you, thank you, but it isn't quite the same thing, is it?"

"It comes to the same thing."

"Does it?"

"Well, sir—"

"Come, come, 'out of' and 'into' aren't the same thing, are they?"

"But they come to the same thing; because there happened to be a reflection."

"So you say. Are you sure you weren't looking at the station or the fields?"

"No, sir."

"I suggest to you that you were. 'Out of' in fact, not 'into'."

"Anyhow I saw the reflection."

"And what was the deceased wearing?"

There was a slight pause while Hardy collected his slow-moving thoughts to meet this new abrupt demand.

"Well, sir, I don't know that I took much notice of his clothes. It was a warm day, and I don't think he had an overcoat. No, I'm sure he hadn't."

"You presume that because it was a warm day he had no overcoat? Isn't that all that it amounts to?" Since Hardy's gesture implied consent, Vernon let it pass and went on: "What coloured suit was he wearing?"

"I think it was brown."

"You *think* it was brown. And what coloured tie? Green?"

"I don't rightly remember."

"I suggest to you that it was red."

"It may have been."

"You aren't very sure about colours, are you? Are you certain that there wasn't a prismatic effect from a flaw in the glass of the window or reflection which made you think there was some colour present which was not in fact there at all?"

"I'm afraid I don't understand all those words, but very likely you're right, sir." Hardy was quite prepared to be friendly with anybody and, having no idea what learned counsel was talking about, was quite ready to agree on a point which seemed to him quite trivial. What did it matter what coloured tie Cargate had been wearing?

"Very likely I *am* right," Vernon went on suavely, and a little contemptuously. "Now, Mr. Hardy, you said, if I heard you rightly, that you noticed a slight flush on Mr. Cargate's face just after he took the snuff. Are you sure that you are right about that too? Might not that be a mistake? Or, alternately, might it not also be due to the fact that you only saw things reflected?"

Put that way it did sound possible and Hardy began to waver. Seeing what he thought was his advantage, Vernon unwisely pressed the point.

"I suggest to you that there was no flush on his face at all."

But by now Hardy had recovered himself and his recollection was clear.

"Yes, sir, there was. I seed it clearly."

"Though you didn't notice the colour of anything else?"

"Well, it changed. Nothing else did."

"Exactly. But the train was moving. The light might have changed too, might it not?"

"Yes sir."

"Thank you, Mr. Hardy." Vernon sat down. It was going to be part of his case that the witness's imagination had played tricks with him, and he thought that he had established his point sufficiently.

In his turn Blayton rose to his feet and addressed the witness. He was not quite sure what Vernon's point was, or how it would help him in view of the medical evidence, but it seemed easy to defeat it. "In your evidence, in chief you said that in your opinion a flush came over the deceased's face just after he took the snuff?"

"Yes, sir."

"I think you said that you clearly saw him take the snuff?"

"Yes, sir."

"And you also said—correct me if I am wrong—that you saw quite clearly that the snuff placed on Mr. Cargate's thumb actually disappeared up his nostril?"

"Yes, sir."

"Thank you, Mr. Hardy." In his turn Blayton expressed his gratitude and resumed his seat. "That will be all, Mr. Hardy."

"Aren't I to say what happened after I pulled the cord and the guard and then Harry Benson and Jim came along? And the engine driver?"

"No, thank you, Mr. Hardy. They can give us quite a clear account of that themselves."

Had Blayton been present at eleven-fifty-eight on that morning, it is doubtful whether he would have been so confident of the clarity of his witnesses, for at the time there is no doubt that there was considerable confusion.

Benson had just recorded that the eleven-fifty-six had, whatever Cargate might have said, left Larkingfield punctually when, as he emerged from his office, he was surprised to hear sounds as if the train were stopping. Looking down the straight track that led away from the station he saw that it had actually stopped.

"Now what's the matter?" he asked himself. "Jim," he called out to the porter. "There ain't any signal against her, is there?"

"Course not. There ain't one there what could be." The porter looked rather pityingly at Benson. The old man must be breaking up, first truckling to men like that—quite unprintable—passenger, and now imagining that a signal had been put up all of a sudden where there never had been one before! "Most likely that man from Scotney End 'All—what's 'is name? Cargate? Most likely he's found something else to complain about. Doesn't like the colour of the cushions, I expect." He relieved his feelings by a loud guffaw.

"Seems as if something 'as 'appened. Guard's going along the line. Better go and see what it is." Benson started to walk down the track, followed by Jim who had nothing to do at the moment that would not wait and was not going to be left out of any fun that there might be. There might be a chance to get his own back on the object of his aversion.

On reaching the train Benson climbed up on to the step outside the carriage while Jim stayed by the side of the track and meditatively picked and chewed a piece of grass.

"Gent been ill." The guard put his head out of the window of the carriage.

"What with? Look of Hardy's face or what?"

"Shut up, Jim. If he should hear you—we're likely to get enough trouble from him as it is. And he said he had a bad heart. Is that it?"

"Very likely." The guard's voice came from inside the carriage; "and if you ask me you aren't to get any more trouble, because I think he's dead."

"Crikey! He can't be. Why, he only just got into the train."

"It was taking the snuff what killed him—if he is dead." Hardy put his head out of the next window.

"Well, what are we going to do about it? Take him out and put him by the side and send for a doctor? We can't keep the train standing here all day. There's two in the front coach as it is and they'll be getting excited; if we don't get on to Great Barwick soon, we'll miss the connection at Luke's Tey."

"Going to be a job getting him out and lowering him down. And if he is a bit dicky it might finish him off."

Benson viewed the practical difficulties. He was less

interested than the guard in such matters as connections with the remote outer world.

"And if he is dead," Hardy put in, "it don't somehow seem right to take him all the way to Great Barwick. Even if he isn't a proper Scotney End man, or even a Larkingfield one, he does sort of belong here and he ought to stay here."

"I could lock up the coach, but it wouldn't help much to take it on if nobody's going to be allowed to get into it. 'Twouldn't be so bad if it weren't a corridor train. No, he'll have to be taken out here. Three of us had better do it while one rings up Great Barwick and tells them what's happened and then perhaps gets on to a doctor. Though if he *is* dead—"

"'Ere," a fresh voice broke in, "are you going to talk all day? 'Cause I want to get on."

Looking out from the window Hardy saw the grimy face of the engine driver below. Instantly all four of those present started to explain to him what the trouble was so that it could not have been easy for him to understand what had happened. But the engine driver was a man of action. He swung himself nimbly up into the train, took one look at Cargate and pronounced a decided, if unscientific opinion that he was entirely dead. Moreover he was quite clear what in his opinion was the right course of action, and having got a definite programme in view, he carried it out regardless of whether it was right or wrong, simply because it was definite.

Carriages, he maintained, containing what he persisted in referring to as "stiffs", ought not to be touched. There had to be an enquiry. Doctors and police and all that sort of thing; "Just in case," he added vaguely.

"You aren't implying, are you," Jim mischievously suggested, "that 'Ardy murdered 'im?"

"Maybe I am and maybe I'm not. Any'ow we drops the

coach 'ere in the siding by the station and while we're doing it, you report to Great Barwick what's 'appened. Then you can settle things up 'ere nice and comfortable at your leisure and the train goes on. Somebody makes a note of this gentleman's address—"

"Mr. Benson and Jim know me," Hardy put in, rather taken aback.

"So much the better. You get in the other coach, then, and there we all are, all serene. Except perhaps the gent what's dead, and even there you can't be sure. Now while I and this young fellow-me-lad with the bright ideas does the shunting, perhaps the stationmaster will do the telephoning."

Chance and the decision of the engine driver had seen to it that some of the evidence as to how Henry Cargate died had not been destroyed, and after an interval, the shortness of which was mainly to the credit of the engine driver, peace once more reigned in Larkingfield Station where nothing moved except the butterflies passing from rose to rose in the beds that flanked the notice-board giving the name of the station. They were very fine roses that Benson grew on the heavy clay soil and they were the pride of his life.

Normally he liked to linger in the complete calm of the platform, for Larkingfield Station lay up a side turning half a mile from the village, and there was nothing to disturb it in between the infrequent trains. But to-day it did not seem to Benson to be at all the same thing. Supposing that man wasn't dead? Supposing he revived and needed attention? He would have no idea of what to do. It would be a great relief when Dr. Gardiner came. If only there was something to do! Jim, unconcernedly, was preparing some food for his dog, but then Jim, apart from the fact that he cared more for his dog than for any human being, was neither in a position of any responsibility nor particularly given to introspection as to sickness or corpses.

Suddenly it had occurred to Benson that he had not done one very obvious thing. He could only imagine that he had forgotten it because the engine driver's ideas—he refused to admit them to be orders—had been otherwise so clear. He had not rung up Scotney End Hall, and he immediately decided to remedy the defect.

The voice of Raikes, the butler, was clear and unruffled and not particularly surprised. He was sorry to hear that Mr. Cargate had been taken unwell. His heart was at all times weak. The doctors had been sent for? That was good. No doubt if it proved to be anything serious Mr. Cargate's own heart specialist would supplement the efforts of the local practitioner who possibly was not aware of the best treatment. What was that? It was suggested that Mr. Cargate was dead? That would indeed be (Raikes had paused as if he found the words difficult to say) very distressing. He would acquaint Miss Knox Forster, Mr. Cargate's secretary, at once. Unfortunately the car being out of action, they had no means of transport, but very likely Miss Knox Forster would decide to make arrangements to come down at once herself. In fact Mr. Benson might assume that that would be so unless he heard to the contrary. Mr. Benson did assume it and it gave him some comfort.

"... These facts, then, will be told to you by the officials of the London and North Eastern Railway Company." Mr. Blayton was now fully in his stride, so much so that Mr. Justice Smith, although he quite agreed that the case ought to be opened very fully indeed, was wondering if he could hint that more matter with less art would be an advantage. But much though he disliked being bored, he disliked even more interrupting counsel who appeared before him.

"Whilst," Mr. Blayton went on serenely unaware of what was passing in his lordship's mind, and indeed intent only upon the jury, "you will of course consider carefully all the evidence which is put before you by myself or by my learned friends who appear for the defence, and only that evidence—for it is my duty to warn you to dismiss from your minds any rumours or previous information which may have reached your ears—you will, I think, concentrate mainly on three points." He breathed a sigh of relief at having successfully reached the conclusion of a sentence which had at one time appeared hopelessly involved and then, raising his fat, podgy fingers successively to enumerate each point in turn, he went on:

"First of all, did Launc—did Henry Cargate die of poison administered to him by means of the snuff? If to that question you return an affirmative answer, the second question which you will have to ask yourself is: 'Was that poison taken voluntarily'—in other words, 'Did the deceased commit suicide, or was it taken accidentally, or was it deliberately placed in the snuff by some person in order to encompass his death?' If in answer to that you reach the conclusion that it was placed there deliberately, then you will have to answer my third point, namely: 'Was that poison placed there by the accused or by some other person?'"

Once more Blayton hitched his gown up on to his shoulders. He was doing, he knew from the faces of the jury, very well. He was getting them interested. He was inducing them to follow him by easy steps so that he was gradually building up in their minds a picture of himself as a reasonable, straightforward, logical man who was trying to help them to arrive at an answer to a difficult problem.

Of the twelve men whom he was addressing—there happened not to be a woman juror—eleven were in fact deeply impressed. Only John Ellis the foreman was a little doubtful whether there was not too much art for the amount of matter, but then, as a Civil Servant, he was rather used to viewing from the other side the particular type of verbiage in which Blayton indulged. Moreover he felt it his duty to be a little more clever than anyone else.

"Of my three points I believe that my first two will not cause you very much difficulty." It was said confidently, but nevertheless Blayton shot a sidelong glance at Vernon and his junior. Surely they were not going to contest the point that Cargate had been murdered by means of the snuff! But not a muscle of Vernon's face moved. It was not until the cross-examination of Hardy was being carried out that he would begin to disclose his defence; perhaps not then, for as yet neither Vernon nor Oliver had seen Hardy and so had not formed any conclusion as to whether it would be worth while trying to shake his evidence.

"Very little difficulty, to my mind." Blayton, having failed to elicit anything from the first statement, repeated it with increased emphasis. It was not very important to know in advance whether the point would be contested, but somehow he felt curious about it. "Very little difficulty, for the medical evidence which will be put before you will be of remarkable clarity. I shall not at this moment worry you with the technical details. Those you will get from Dr. Gardiner, who arrived very soon after the tragedy had occurred and very properly refused to certify the cause of death without a more detailed examination, and from the pathologist and analyst who were subsequently called upon to give the police the benefit of their expert knowledge. Their evidence must of necessity be in some respects technical, but I think that with a little care, you and I, members of the jury, will be able to understand it. At any rate we will try to do so—together."

Ellis looked up at the Judge and wondered whether behind that learned and inscrutable face with its aquiline nose, lurked a brain which resented Mr. Blayton's oratorical arts as deeply as he did.

"But before I say more I will call to your attention the correctness of the behaviour of Dr. Gardiner. One accident alone was responsible for the death of Henry Cargate and two pieces of care alone have made it possible for any enquiry into his death to be carried out. I have already referred to the action of the London and North Eastern Railway Company—that was one of the pieces of care. The accident was simply that there happened to be a wasps' nest near to Scotney End Hall, the residence of the deceased; a simple but annoying wasps' nest which Henry Cargate had instructed his gardener to destroy, and for which purpose he had himself made a purchase of a quantity, an unnecessarily large quantity, for he was rather ignorant of what was required, of a suitable substance. That, as you will see, was the accident which caused his death. But the second piece of care was the thoroughness with which Dr. Gardiner acted, and that for a patient whom he had not attended before and whom he could never attend again."

He paused dramatically and Mr. Justice Smith took the opportunity to sneeze, thus rather spoiling the effect. Unfortunately, too, for Anstruther Blayton, although the majority of the witnesses had been excluded in the normal manner from the Court, there still remained the Inspector in charge of the case and the medical witnesses. Therefore, as he listened to the opening speech for the Crown, Inspector Fenby imperceptibly shrugged his shoulders and good humouredly thought that there were other people concerned. "In any case," his reflections went on, "it was the engine driver, not the railway company, who was responsible, and even in his case his principal motive was to get his train on to Great Barwick and ultimately finish his day's work."

But Dr. Gardiner, also listening by the courtesy of the Court to what Blayton had to say, blushed more with shame than with pleasure, for he was an honest man who had no desire to receive credit that was not his due, and he had to admit to himself that when he gave the account on which Blayton was basing his speech, he had left out what nearly happened. He might so easily have slipped up in the sunlit station yard at Larkingfield with the deep red and orange roses flanked with mignonette scenting the whole air. It had not been very easy to notice any other smell.

At first it had seemed perfectly simple. He was busy at the time. One of Hardy's cousins, a numerous tribe, had succeeded in jabbing the fork with which he was cleaning out a pigsty into his foot, and the resultant wound was none too clean. After dressing that, Gardiner had hurried back to his own surgery in Larkingfield, expecting to find that before he could deal with those of his patients who had come round to him there, he would be called away to a confinement at Hinstead, seven miles away on the opposite side of Larkingfield to Scotney End. Consequently he was not pleased when he was summoned to the station.

Moreover, Cargate was a man for whom he had no reason to go out of his way. Like Hardy he resented the way in which the owner of Scotney End Hall got everything he could from London, only that in his case the cause of friction was not bread, but medical advice. Then, too, the way in which Cargate had let the latter fact be known was not exactly tactful according to the account given by the vicar of Scotney End who had rather needlessly retailed it to Gardiner. For Cargate was not only rich, he was purse proud, and he let everybody know that economy was unnecessary to him, so that when the vicar, intending to do a good turn to both Cargate and Gardiner had commented on how fortunate it was, in view of Cargate's weak heart, that the local practitioner was an excellent up-to-date man, Cargate had cut him short at once.

"I should never go to any one like that, *I* believe in getting the best advice. Even if I couldn't afford it, I should never dream of practising economy in that kind of way. No, I'm quite prepared to pay my own doctor to come down from London when I need him and bring a decent heart specialist with him if he thinks it advisable."

The poor vicar had felt rather snubbed, unnecessarily snubbed, and perhaps it was in a spirit not quite up to the level of his usually high Christian principles that he let Gardiner know that he need expect no addition to his practice so far as the owner of Scotney End Hall was concerned. "Though of course there might be the staff," he had added, "and Miss Knox Forster, but she, I understand, is never ill."

"Plenty to do already," Gardiner had growled, "though I freely admit that I like having the rich patients to help pay for the poor and Cargate, if he has as weak a heart as you say he has, might have been a very useful annuity."

"Well, as to his health, I'm only repeating what he says. Don't take it from me." The vicar was always a lover of accuracy.

At the time Gardiner had only smiled. He was not in the habit of accepting any diagnosis at second-hand in that way. But as he hurried to Larkingfield Station, it whimsically occurred to him that now he *might* take it from the vicar. For if, as Benson seemed to think, Cargate was dead already, it would save a great deal of trouble if he could sign a certificate that death was due to heart failure.

"Where have you got him, Benson?" he asked. "Not still in the carriage over there? My good man! With the sun blazing on him! Didn't you do anything to make him comfortable?" Gardiner remembered his feelings rather grimly when subsequently he read Blayton's comments on the courtesy and acumen of the London and North Eastern Railway.

But after all it was a little harsh to blame Benson for not knowing exactly what to do. Besides he had, in fact, done what he could. The blinds of the compartment were drawn, Cargate's collar had been loosened and he had been laid down full length on the seat with an improvised cushion under his head.

It did not take Gardiner very long to see that it was of no real importance what the stationmaster had or had not done. There was no question but that Cargate was dead, and from what he could understand of the story which Benson had told him of what Hardy had seen and done he had probably died instantaneously.

There was, too, in Gardiner's mind, very little doubt about the cause of death. There must, he presumed, be a more detailed examination by himself or by someone else, but it was fairly clear what the result would be. A weak heart, an outburst of bad temper, perhaps a slight jerk as the train started. It might have happened at any time and the pinch of snuff was probably nothing but a coincidence. It was another of those very frequent cases when the lay mind would fasten on the non-essential but very visible detail that was really irrelevant. So far as he could see, too, the signs were all those that should accompany heart failure. Yes, no doubt that was the cause. He would quite cheerfully at that moment have signed a certificate of death by natural causes owing to heart failure, only he was not Cargate's doctor and he had not attended on him recently or at any time, and therefore he could do nothing so simple. He was just going to get out of the carriage when his eye by chance fell on the snuffbox.

Cargate had apparently been sitting in the corner on the left facing the engine, the corridor being on his right-hand side. The snuffbox had apparently been in his right hand and as he fell back it had fallen from his grasp. In fact it must have been almost thrown forward, for it now lay partly under the seat on the other side, a yard to the right of where Cargate had been sitting. Whether it had been open or not when it fell of course Gardiner did not know, but anyhow it had flown open when it fell and it was now upside down. Gardiner could see a little pile of light brown powder on the floor underneath it.

It looked rather an interesting box, made undoubtedly of gold, and on the lid was some design in emeralds and rubies but with, or so it appeared, a large gap where the central stone should have been. It was an attractive piece of workmanship. Gardiner wondered whether he ought to touch it. At any rate he might stoop down to examine it better without committing any impropriety. The result was, as he might have expected, a violent sneeze that disturbed the brown powder. Gardiner straightened himself up. His nose seemed to be tingling almost painfully and the smell of the mignonette from outside seemed stronger than ever. He put a handkerchief to his nose and rubbed it in a manner reminiscent, had he but known it, of Jim's dog when he too had encountered some of the contents of the same box.

It seemed to him curious, but before he could do anything more about it, Benson's voice came from outside.

"Here's Miss Knox Forster, sir, Mr. Cargate's secretary. And if, sir, when you've settled what to do, you wouldn't mind telling me, I shall be glad; because I didn't ought to keep this coach here much longer. For one thing the company will be wanting the use of it, maybe. And for another I've got two trucks due to come into that siding to-morrow and there isn't another one hereabouts. So if I could be free to arrange to have that coach moved—"

"I quite understand, Benson, and I'll let you know as soon as I can. All the same—" he seemed to change his mind and turned to the woman who had just arrived, "there isn't any need to keep him here. What would you like done about it? I'm sorry, I ought to have introduced myself. My name is Gardiner. I'm the local doctor. Benson rang me up and got me to come here. I'm afraid that Mr. Cargate has died suddenly in the train. We ought to move him somewhere and then get on to his relations."

"Yes. But Scotney End Hall's the best part of five miles away and our car's broken down. I got here on a bicycle."

"I see. Of course we could use my car as an ambulance. But, if you prefer it, perhaps my surgery would be a good place? Though I don't particularly want to give up the space and I certainly don't want to press it because, if an examination must be done, I'm not his doctor."

The woman who faced him seemed to sense something of the soreness lying behind the simple statement of fact. She altered the weight of her tall body from one foot to the other, while a puzzled expression came into the steel-blue eyes that looked out unflinchingly from under her grey hair.

"The whole thing is a little complicated. So far as I know

Mr. Cargate has no relations in the world and I don't know who his executors are. I suppose really they ought to make the decisions."

"Perhaps. But meanwhile—"

"It wouldn't take long to get on to his solicitors. He told me that his will was with them and before I came down here, I took a note of their telephone number. We could ring up from here."

Gardiner looked at his watch.

"They'll probably all be out to lunch by now; it's just after one." He felt quite relieved to have thought of something which this extremely competent woman had apparently overlooked. He found Miss Knox Forster a little overpowering, and he had once more fallen back into indecisiveness as he went on: "I don't somehow quite like leaving him here and I can't stay. I've got much too much to do."

"Obviously I can stay. In a sense my occupation has ended. I think it's worth while seeing if those solicitors are in and how soon it will be before some authorized person can get on the scene. If it will be some time, then I agree that we must move him, to clear the station if for no other reason; but if not, a few hours wouldn't matter. Do you mind hanging on for a few minutes while I ring these solicitors up?"

Gardiner could do nothing but consent. A very sweeping, rather abrupt and domineering woman, Miss Knox Forster, he had thought as he watched her stride rather clumsily but quickly along to the stationmaster's office. Having nothing to do he started to walk about and presently, finding himself by Benson's flower-beds, he stooped down and put his nose into one of the deep crimson blooms. Then he straightened himself up suddenly with a jerk, a startled expression on his face, then he stooped again, lower down this time, till he was sniffing the mignonette. A second later and he was hurrying back to the carriage as fast as he could go, searching in his pocket as he went for an envelope sufficiently durable for his purpose. A bad habit of carrying about with him unread correspondence unjustly assisted him to find what he wanted.

Long before Miss Knox Forster had put through her call, he had gone into the carriage and swept up some of the light brown powder that lay on the floor. There was no doubt about it, the smell that permeated the carriage was *not* that of rose or mignonette. Was it perhaps faintly reminiscent of almonds? If so, it suggested a curious and entirely new idea to his brain. It might, of course, be nothing more than ordinary snuff, but now that he looked at it again it seemed to him to be a *very* light brown. He wasn't sure. He might be quite wrong, but there could be no harm in seeing that no facts were lost.

The only question really was how much more ought he to try to preserve. If he was more certain, perhaps he ought to insist on the whole coach being kept *in status quo*. But he was not. And suddenly he decided to keep his opinions to himself, or rather to divulge them only to the proper authority, and not, for instance, to the stationmaster or to Miss Knox Forster.

So, unobtrusively, he got out of the carriage again, just in time so that that decided lady, when she finished her telephone conversation, was not to know that he had ever left the track and the platform.

"I've got through to the solicitors," she said cheerfully. "All the partners were of course, as you thought, out to lunch. It seems to me sometimes that you men, especially business ones, give rather an undue prominence to that meal. However, I had a certain amount of luck. Usually one finds that no one is about but a half-witted office boy, but this time there was a managing clerk, and as he happened to have dealt with Mr. Cargate's will, of course he knew all about it. Naturally too he wanted to be extremely secretive. I suppose they think that it sounds important."

"But you got something out of him?"

"Yes, after a short argument. The sole executor is the senior partner of this particular firm and my managing clerk believed that he would consent to act. Power, he was careful to explain, had been given in the will for them to charge their ordinary fees, which, if I know anything of my late employer, will be better described as extraordinary."

"So I gathered."

"Well, he *was* rather like that. He never thought that he was getting good value unless he was overcharged, but I must say that he did generally go to good people."

It occurred to Gardiner to wonder how much Miss Knox Forster herself had been in the habit of overcharging her employer for her probably very efficient services, and quick as lightning she answered his thought.

"Oh, yes! I got the job by asking half as much salary again as anyone else who applied. I think that I've been worth it—otherwise I should have got the sack long ago. You had to give value, I must say. But that's beside the point. This firm of solicitors—Anderson and Ley—are apparently very well known—"

"I have heard of them. They've got rather a reputation."

"I'm not surprised. Apparently also they are very busy. Mr. Ley is extremely unlikely, according to his managing clerk, to be able to come down till to-morrow. I've said that I'll ring them up again later. I thought of making them ring me up but I don't know whether I shall be here or have gone back to Scotney End. I can put through a personal call and so get Ley pretty well as soon as he comes back from lunch, but meanwhile it does make it awkward."

"It does," Gardiner agreed. "You know I don't think that there's any point in keeping him in that coach."

"I'm ready to take your advice about that, but if you think that he ought to be moved, on the whole I think it would be better if we took him back to Scotney End. There'll be room there," she added grimly.

"Very well, then. I'll do that and then, in a way, I retire from the case unless you want me. But I can't certify the cause of death; at least not without consultation with his own doctor. As a matter of fact I think that I ought to talk to the coroner."

"If you've got the time—"

"I must make it somehow."

"I wish you would. You know about these things and I don't. You could explain it much better."

Gardiner nodded.

"You can take that as settled. Will you start going back to Scotney End to warn them there? Or would you prefer to come with me and bring your bicycle later?"

"We may want some help to carry him upstairs. Raikes is rather old and that only leaves you and me and the gardener and the maids. I shall ring up from here and tell them to expect us while you and the stationmaster and the porter get him into the back of your car. The door will come off the lamp-shed quite easily, by the way. Then I shall go back with you, and I shall get the porter to ride my bicycle up and give us a hand. He can hold on to the back of the car for that distance, whatever the Road Traffic Act may say, and perhaps you will bring him back. Meanwhile," Miss Knox

Forster swept on, "shall I take that snuffbox or will you put it in his pocket?"

"Perhaps I'd better take it."

"Just as you like, though I don't see why. Be careful of it, though, it's rather valuable—even though the central stone is missing."

"So I noticed, but I shan't steal it," Gardiner laughed, "though I'm glad to hear that you know about the stone. My taking it is only a formality—in case the coroner wants to see it."

"As an *objet d'art,* he might like it, but I can't see why he should otherwise. However, let's get hold of the stationmaster."

Gardiner called out to Benson and explained what was wanted. His own experience made him a little doubtful as to whether Miss Knox Forster's sweeping plans for employing all the station staff would be accomplished quite so easily as she seemed to expect, but somehow, rather to Gardiner's surprise, everybody fell in line with the proposals which she put forward, always politely, but with a manner that definitely presumed that there would be no hitch in their execution.

The transference to the car was affected without any serious trouble, though with more exertion than was really pleasant on so hot a day. Just as Gardiner was about to drive off, Benson came up with one more question to ask.

"I suppose, sir, that there's no reason for keeping the coach where it is any longer?"

For a second Gardiner hesitated.

"No, I don't think so," he answered slowly.

"I don't know why," Miss Knox Forster put in, "but it smelt to me awfully frowsty and heady. Musty, as it were."

Benson looked offended.

"The company washes all its coaches out thoroughly every day."

"Then that will be washed out to-night?"

"Undoubtedly, sir. Unless you say that it should not be. And then perhaps I ought to give a reason."

"N-no," Gardiner hesitated. "I think it may be. In fact I think that I should do so pretty thoroughly. It will be done to-night, you say?"

"Yes, sir, or we may arrange to have it done here ourselves."

"I see. Yes. Thank you." Gardiner's mind seemed to be wandering and he still seemed absent-minded as he drove his car slowly out of the station yard with Jim hanging on behind. It was not until Miss Knox Forster spoke to him that he seemed to remember what he was doing.

"Now why on earth did you say 'Wash it thoroughly'?"

"Oh, I don't know. Mightn't be nice for other people if they didn't." It seemed a very vague answer.

The conversation stopped abruptly, even though there was no need for Gardiner to concentrate very closely on his driving in the empty and well-known by-road.

Scotney End, it occurred to him, was an out-of-the-way place for anyone of Cargate's temperament to have selected. Men of his type usually went to a better known or more populous district, Surrey, for instance, and spoke of East Anglia in terms of faint contempt. But probably Scotney End Hall had itself been the attraction.

It certainly was very lovely with its warm red Tudor brick basking in the midday sun, the weathervane, high up on the roof, barely moving in the gentle breeze. The drive gate was open and they soon crossed over the moat that encircled the house on three sides, with tall elms standing on its banks, and past the low wall that surrounded the garden. To their left, in a long herbaceous border, the last of the lupins and delphiniums lingered, and the hollyhocks stood tall and many coloured, while on the other side the peach, nectarine and apricot trees showed the promise of a plentiful crop. Beyond were lawns, strangely enough not well kept, and the promise of shade from more fine trees.

"How one gardener kept it all up in the old days, I don't know," Miss Knox Forster remarked. "I suppose the people who were here did a good deal themselves, but even so—We were going to get some more people but gardeners aren't easy to find if you want good ones. And there was difficulty too about getting a cottage for anyone."

"I know. It doesn't matter saying it now, but the people here thought you ought to have employed local people, so they weren't anxious to make it easy for you by letting you have any accommodation at all."

"Surly. And cutting their own throats really. But I believe you're right; it's rather what the vicar implied."

"Yockleton? He's a good chap really, but a bit crusty if you get the wrong side of him."

"Which Mr. Cargate had—thoroughly. In fact they had a frightful quarrel yesterday. In which, so far as I can make out, Mr. Yockleton was entirely in the right."

"Was he? Well, here we are." Gardiner had apparently no desire to discuss the point and Joan Knox Forster, with a little pout, got out of the car. She had no particular desire to describe what had passed between her employer and the vicar but she did not like being sent about her business so obviously. However, there was no denying the fact that they had arrived at Scotney End Hall and that Raikes was coming out of the front door.

The butler seemed to be unnecessarily agitated and came up to Joan Knox Forster at once.

"I'm sorry, Miss, but I simply couldn't do it."

"Do what?"

"Help carry him up." He seemed to find it difficult even to say the words.

Gardiner turned to him abruptly.

"But you've got to. It'll take four of us. You can't expect Miss Knox Forster to make one."

"I'm sorry, sir, but I'm not as strong as I used to be."

The doctor looked at him carefully. It certainly was true that he was past middle-age, but all the same he looked as if he ought to be capable of making the effort. Probably there was more truth in the broken sentences which he was now muttering about never having been able to bring himself to go near anything—anything like that. He glanced at the rug that covered what was in the back of the car and practically fled. His face seemed strangely white and unhappy to the doctor, whose own feelings on the subject had been hardened so long ago that he was incapable of remembering that they had ever been otherwise.

"He's rather an old fool," Miss Knox Forster commented drily, "but I didn't think that he was quite so stupid as that. It's a good thing that you didn't jolt our friend here too badly so that he's got here safely." She pointed to Jim who was standing a little sheepishly by the wall of the house against which he had rested Miss Knox Forster's bicycle—or to be accurate, the one which she had borrowed. He didn't like riding a woman's bicycle, and that was a fact.

However, before it was necessary for him to say anything, the one gardener whom Cargate had managed to retain at Scotney End appeared from round the corner of the house and, with Miss Knox Forster proving herself quite capable of carrying out the task which Raikes had refused, the remains of Henry Cargate were soon placed in peace on his own bed.

It had been a strange scene, Gardiner thought, as he drove off, for no one so far as he could make out, had pretended throughout to show the slightest signs of sorrow, for it could not be suggested that grief had been the cause of Raikes's emotion. Indeed, it had seemed more like repugnance. There was no particular reason of course why any of them should have been distressed. After all, no one who had been there had been a friend, let alone a relation, and that perhaps was the real tragedy of Cargate's life—that he was surrounded only by employees, by those whose assistance he had bought. Gardiner wondered if that were equally true of Cargate's friendships. Somehow he thought that it was, and for the first time he felt sorry for the man.

But he had no time to waste in indulging in such speculation. Soon there would be his temporarily neglected practice to attend to—he was getting hungry too and he had an unpleasant suspicion that he might find that there was no time for him to have any food. Above all he had to make a decision before he dropped Jim at Larkingfield Station. Was he to allow his recommendation as to the cleaning and removal of the coach to stand, or was he to countermand it? Assuming, that was, that Benson was still prepared to take his orders.

Making decisions as to his own conduct was at all times difficult to Dr. Gardiner, although he had to do so every day for other people. Often he would have liked to have had a second opinion before advising some treatment, even before prescribing a simple medicine, and if the advice he was giving involved a course of action, such as undergoing an operation, which, once done, could not be undone, his state of mind became almost pitiable. Perhaps he ought never to have taken up such a profession as medicine; almost certainly his vacillation had prevented him from having any chance of reaching the front rank of it.

He was still trying to decide when he found himself once more at Larkingfield Station, at the foot of the turning to which Benson was standing, signalling to him not to turn off the road on which he was.

"Get out at once, Jim. Quickly. You're wanted as fast as ever you can go at Hinstead, Doctor; surgery has just rung up to say 'Baby coming'."

Before Gardiner had quite realized what he was doing, he found that he was driving on and that Benson and the porter were out of sight. Very well, then; fate had made the decision for him. Perhaps it would be all right. After all he had the snuffbox, the envelope and its contents. Moreover, the Coroner did not live such a long way from Hinstead.

"I beg your pardon, Mr. Blayton, I hope I didn't interrupt you." Mr. Justice Smith recovered from his fit of sneezing. "You were saying?"

"Not at all, my lord. I was referring to the care and intelligence of Dr. Gardiner. He will be here later to give you his evidence"—Blayton got into his stride again—"and he will tell you how from the very first moment he doubted whether Henry Cargate's death was in reality the simple case of heart failure that to a less astute person it might have appeared. His doubts were instantly aroused by the aroma in the carriage which he immediately detected as quite different from that of the flowers which happened to be close to the window of the carriage in which the unfortunate deceased man was. That smell was familiar to Dr. Gardiner. It at once reminded him of what, as you will hear later, it turned out to be—potassium cyanide, a deadly poison to men as well as to wasps. With that Dr. Gardiner's mind was made up with a rapidity and a decisiveness which must be characteristic of the man. And thereupon he acted, straightaway, and with skill and forethought."

In the jury box John Ellis put his left hand under his chin and tugged at the flesh underneath, a habit which certainly was characteristic of *him* when he wanted to express mild doubt and disapproval. To himself he murmured a single line of verse: "The carpenter said nothing but 'The butter's spread too thick'." But a glance at the eleven other jurymen made him suspect that it was not too thick for them. He alone of the jury was not fully East Anglian, a district which was to him just a dormitory. But the others were glad to hear so much praise of a local man, more especially as they were well aware that "those London police" had been called in instead of their own constabulary, and they were inclined to think that that was a mistake. Therefore, they breathed heavily and prepared to welcome Blayton's further remarks.

The effect was not lost on counsel for the Crown (for Ellis alone was in any way capable of concealing his opinions) and therefore he went on happily:

"The action which Dr. Gardiner took was to retain the snuffbox and to procure quite a quantity of the powder on the floor, so that the one could subsequently be analysed, and the other examined and such traces of snuff as lingered in it, be also analysed. Moreover, he achieved all this in such a manner that no one, neither the station officials nor Miss Knox Forster were aware that he had done so, and therefore everyone both at the station and at Scotney End Hall, including even the accused, was for some while under the happy impression that with the washing of the coach every trace of the crime had been removed. And note that Dr. Gardiner suggested to the stationmaster that that should be done, and did so publicly, since he knew that everything of value had been removed from the carriage without anyone knowing that that had been done.

"Having thus acted, as I have said, with forethought, decision and promptitude, Dr. Gardiner then took the snuff-box and the envelope containing the precious sample of the powder to the Coroner of the district and communicated to him what he knew. He pointed out that, although he had not analysed the powder, he had the very gravest suspicion of it, and with that he considered very properly that the matter was out of his hands. In due course the Chief Constable was notified, and decided for reasons which need not concern us, to call in the assistance of Scotland Yard. Of the action which they took you will hear in due course from Inspector Fenby.

"We shall submit to you, in accordance with the statement of the butler, that the particular snuffbox was cleaned out on the morning of Thursday, July 12th, and that snuff, fresh from a new tin, was placed in it at that time, and that therefore we have only to consider who could have had access between the morning of July 12th, and the time when Mr. Cargate set off for Larkingfield railway station. Actually, as you will hear, that time can be very much shortened since the bottle containing the crystals was only out of Mr. Cargate's own sight for one long and three short periods during the day until he handed it over to his gardener at approximately 5 p.m. that evening, after which time you will learn from the gardener's evidence that no one could have laid hands on it except the gardener himself, and that he could not have had access to the snuffbox.

"Unless therefore we have to deal with collusion between the gardener and some other person, an improbable, though not impossible proposition, for those who are about to commit murder seldom take anyone else into their confidence, we shall only have to deal with a few minutes round 11.15 in the morning, a further few at 11.30, the whole of the time between 12 noon and 1.45 p.m., and a few minutes around 3.30 p.m. That is primarily, for you will find that there is an important exception to that statement.

"Nevertheless, members of the jury, I want you to bear those times in mind, for each of them is important as giving a particular person an opportunity to obtain the potassium cyanide, and in fairness I must deal with each of them, since it is very likely that my learned friend who appears for the defence will suggest to you that those periods of time provided an opportunity when some other person than the accused might have tampered with the potassium cyanide and the snuff.

"Very possibly, too, he will suggest to you that those other persons had also motives for wishing Henry Cargate to die, motives rather smacking perhaps of altruism but still, some sort of motives. And here let me confess to you," Mr. Blayton managed to look almost too honest to be true, "that the processes of thought actuating all those concerned, including the accused, almost reflect credit upon them. It would appear that everyone at Scotney End was full of excellent intentions, even if those intentions led them to contemplate murder. For let me also confess that Henry Cargate had not a perfect character. His first name, which at his lordship's desire, I have not troubled you with greatly, happened to be Launcelot. But it could not have been Galahad. If it had it would not have been in keeping with his character, for though we are not, happily, concerned with matters of sex, it could not be said that his heart was pure." Mr. Blayton paused sorrowfully and shook his head before going on slowly.

"But, gentlemen of the jury, it is not permitted to murder even the most wicked of men.

"These points," seeing the ghost of a smile hovering around the mouth of the foreman of the jury, he went on rapidly, "will be brought to your notice more fully in the evidence which will be put before you. It will be my duty to show why in the opinion of the Crown, though several people had the opportunity and the desire, only one person actually put these intentions into practice. Moreover, I have to prove that that person is the accused and to build step by step the facts which have been ascertained and which have led us to that conclusion, and by which I shall endeavour to lead you to a similar conclusion."

Part II

Investigation

It was all very well for Anstruther Blayton to talk as if he, with perhaps a little assistance from his junior, had been wholly responsible for all the work of building up the facts on which the prosecution was based but, while he had every right to claim that he had decided what evidence should be put forward and how it ought to be presented, he might have indicated faintly that some work had been done by the County Police, by Inspector Fenby, and by Scotland Yard.

It had seemed first of all a perfectly simple case to Fenby, and even if the local police were unduly busy at the moment, the reason which the Chief Constable had given for an apparently reluctant decision to call in Scotland Yard, he thought that they ought to have been able to deal with it themselves.

But it was never his habit to jump to conclusions and he expected that there would probably be a little more to it than just finding out who had purchased the potassium cyanide, which would only be a routine matter of searching the poison register of a number of chemists, perhaps only of quite a small number.

For the brief particulars which had been given to him

made no bones of Cargate having died as the result of taking poison absorbed through the mucous membrane in taking snuff. There was so much potassium cyanide in the sample which Dr. Gardiner had obtained and handed to the Coroner that the only wonder was that Cargate himself had not noticed either its smell or its appearance; but the Chief Constable had heard that it had been taken by an angry man thoughtlessly, and he pronounced that this was the reason why it had not been detected. The analysis was as yet not made, but it would not be surprising if it emerged that about a third of the snuff had been removed and potassium cyanide substituted. Moreover the analyst was inclined to think, judging only from a preliminary investigation which would need confirming, that the crystals had been ground up so as to blend more readily with the brown powder. Also, of course, they could be more readily absorbed if they were in that form.

All this was quite straightforward, but when the Chief Constable went on to say that the purchase of the poison had been traced, Fenby felt at once that he was going to be told something which would show that the case was not quite so simple after all. And sure enough, his intuition turned out to be correct, for the poison had been bought quite openly in Great Barwick and for a quite legitimate purpose by the man whose death it had caused.

"So that," the Chief Constable went on, "one of two things has happened. Either he has deliberately committed suicide, which there is no reason to suspect. Or he inadvertently put temptation in someone's way. In other words it is not a premeditated crime. I don't think, by the way, that it can possibly be an accident. Not if those crystals are ground up."

Fenby could only agree, even if rather sorrowfully. Unpremeditated crimes were, in his experience, either so obvious that a child could solve them or else chance had put such an opportunity in the way of the murderer that detection became the very devil because there was nothing from which to work.

It looked horribly as if this crime was going to fall into that category, in which case the Chief Constable had a better reason than had at first been apparent when he switched the responsibility over to Scotland Yard. Fenby felt already a strong dislike for rich men who inconsiderately purchased poison by which they themselves met their own end. It could only be called downright careless. Then he brightened up. If those crystals had been ground, there ought to be something to be found out about how that was done. Moreover, that was not quite unpremeditated.

However, it was no time for meditative reflections. It was a time for action, and the first thing to do was to see Ley and warn him that there would be delays before he could arrange for the funeral, let alone prove the will of his client. There might, too, be something to be deduced from the contents of that will.

The "senior partner of Messrs. Anderson and Ley" had somehow coined up in Fenby's mind the vision of an elderly, solemn, perhaps rather pedantic man, full of precedents and dignity, and quite unlikely to be willing to step from the paths of correctitude sufficiently to be really helpful. Consequently Fenby was slightly taken aback when he found himself shown in to a man of rather under middle age, very sharp and alert, extremely talkative, and quick to see every point that was coming almost before it was made.

"Scotland Yard in connection with my very recently deceased client? Quick work, Inspector." Ley had greeted him cheerfully. "We only got a telephone call through from Cargate's secretary this morning—while I was out to lunch, in fact. How did he die? When I rang up Miss Knox Forster this afternoon and arranged to go down to-morrow, I understood her to say that it was heart failure."

"It may have been, sir, and it may not. It's because it may not that I'm here."

"I see." Ley whistled. "I suppose you aren't going to tell me anything more but you want to know a good deal from me?"

"Exactly." Fenby saw no use in wasting words in modifying what was precisely his attitude. It was a perfectly reasonable wish on his part and he saw that Ley quite understood it. It was one of the reasons for Fenby's success that he summed up people quickly and knew who needed urging and who could be allowed to go on in his own way.

"I suppose," Ley went on, "that you've found out that I'm the sole executor?"

"Yes."

"Now I wonder how? My clerk told Miss Knox Forster this morning, and I suppose you've been in touch with her."

"Not directly. She told the doctor and he told us. That's putting it briefly. But actually Miss Knox Forster and everyone else at Scotney End Hall is unaware, I am given to understand, that Cargate did not die naturally. They know there may have to be a Coroner's inquest, but they do not know that we are interested, and on the whole I think it would be better if they did not—at any rate just at present. Assuming that he was murdered, and assuming that it was done by someone in or around the house, then that somebody must be interviewed and he or she had better be in ignorance of who is conducting the interview. Even Miss Knox Forster had better not be told or she may unconsciously put him or her on her guard. Whereas, if she knows nothing—"

"I see. Then you want me as executor to say nothing and more or less do nothing?"

"That's about what it comes to. There will have to be a post-mortem and an inquest, and if you wouldn't mind just falling into line with anything we suggest?"

"Certainly. I won't try to arrange a cremation. And nobody else is interested."

"Thank you. But, *nobody*? Aren't there any relations?"

"Who might have murdered him for his money? None at all."

"Not even anyone who might have hoped to have been left something?"

"Quantities of acquaintances and other hopeful people. A rich man like Cargate, even when as unattractive as he was, is bound to collect hangers-on of the worst sort when he has a weak heart and no relations. His doctor, for instance, always made a tremendous fuss of him and I'm sure is full of hope of receiving some compensation for losing so valuable an annuity. But he won't get a penny and I must say that I should like to see his face when he hears it—oily, plausible scoundrel." Ley grinned cheerfully. "Competent, though. Wouldn't kill him by accident. In fact I should say had kept him alive for a great many years longer that was strictly necessary—or desirable."

Seeing that the solicitor was getting away from the point, Fenby thought that he had better bring him back to it. Besides he had as yet no knowledge of Cargate's character and so he was almost shocked to hear him spoken of in this way.

"But somebody must be his heir. If there is a will, he can't be intestate."

"What makes you think that?" Ley became mildly sarcastic at Fenby's expense. "He's got as near to it as he can. The will appoints me as executor, it gives power to us to make our usual professional charges. We had, by the way, some difficulty in persuading him not to insist on the word 'overcharges'. It might have led to difficulties, so we have put 'at the excessive scale which we have been in the habit of charging him', or some such words which, by the way, are dubious law. The will is full of insults of that kind."

"Which you haven't resented so far as you are concerned?"

"Not in the least. Anybody can insult me as much as he chooses at a sufficiently high rate. Besides I frankly told Cargate that I charged him as much as possible, or a trifle more, but that I was well worth it. It was the only way to get his confidence. I even ended up one small account of a number of petty items which mounted up to just over sixty pounds by writing the words 'Say eighty-four guineas' at the end. And he paid. It was the only joke I ever knew him appreciate. But to get back, Inspector, to where I was when you induced me to go off at this tangent. He insisted on including reasons why he does not propose to grant legacies to me or anybody else—somewhat vitriolic reasons—and then he has gone on to be rude to a few charities who had approached him for subscriptions. I rather resented that but I couldn't get him to leave it out, so there it is. It's rather stupid, but I couldn't help it."

"And what finally has he done with it?"

"Left it all to the nation."

"Of all the dull and undeserving—"

"Precisely. He held the economic view that money paid to the nation in any form, taxes or gifts, was always wasted and did nobody any good, and he wanted to do nobody any good. At one time he thought of putting up shower baths in the North Pole or Turkish ones in the Sahara, but then he dropped that as being childish. He very nearly left it to be divided equally between Germany, Italy, Japan, the Irish

Free State and the Republic of San Marino. But that would have been a nuisance, so I stopped it."

"I see." Fenby spoke very slowly. "Was he by any chance quite sane?"

"Not much madder than most other people. You won't, by the way, be able to contest the will on the ground that leaving everything of which you die possessed to the nation is an obvious sign of lunacy. It'll be called patriotism, which is only nearly the same thing and quite different in law."

"I wasn't thinking of contesting it," Fenby answered a little crossly.

"No, I don't expect you were, but if you hated everyone in the world, what would you do? It's difficult to think of a good joke or of anyone who will be embarrassed by being left a million or so. If they were likely to be, they need not take it, for one thing."

But Fenby refused to follow the solicitor into such realms of fancy. Besides, he had by now achieved everything for which he came and he had no desire to plunge himself into a morass of economic theory and consider whether Cargate's money would be benefiting everybody, as would certainly be represented by the Press, or nobody, as was apparently Cargate's own opinion.

"In a sense, I suppose," thought Fenby, "it *is* a diminishment of purchasing power, therefore deflation, and therefore a bad thing. I give it up. Economics were always too much for me, but thank goodness I don't have to try to understand them. I only know that the nation has got to pay for the expenses of the car that is going to take me down to Great Barwick to-night and then, less obtrusively, to see Dr. Gardiner, and that Cargate's cash can do it nicely. I wish he'd left it towards increasing the salaries of police officers—with a personal grant to anyone who discovered how he was murdered. But people never seem to think of such delicate attentions before they go off and get themselves killed. So there it is."

The doctor, when Fenby eventually reached him, was legitimately tired and rather disinclined to enter at length into the subject which had brought Fenby there but, sincerely though the Inspector thought it a monstrous imposition that he should be made to do so, he had to be induced to give a full account of what had happened because there was no denying that anyone concerned with Scotney End Hall or its neighbourhood might come under suspicion, and that Gardiner had been in a position to see their first reactions to the news, an opportunity which of course could only possibly occur once.

He was, moreover, himself quick to see the point and it took very little tact on Fenby's part to get him to talk, and when he did so, he proved to be of genuine assistance, for he first of all gave his story fully and without comment, and then ended by a few of his own reflections.

"In a way, you know," he said, "I am very glad to get all this off my chest for two reasons. First of all, did I do the right thing in letting that carriage be cleaned?"

Privately Fenby had his own doubts, but it would have been almost cruel to have voiced them. "I think so," he said. "I don't imagine that there was anything more to be found out from it. Of course in theory—" Then seeing that Gardiner was looking anxiously at him, he went on hurriedly: "No, on the whole, I think it was best. At any rate there may be compensating advantages."

"Which brings me to my second reason for wanting to tell you all about it. At least I think that it does. I've had a nasty feeling all day that I wasn't being quite honest. You see I let everybody think that in my opinion Cargate had died quite a natural death and all the time, or rather most of the time, I was almost certain that he had not. Consequently when Raikes turned and fled, and when Miss Knox Forster let slip that there had been a row between Cargate and Yockleton, I couldn't help noticing it and at the same time I didn't like it. It's all very well for you. It's your business, but it isn't mine, and I felt that I was in a false position."

"Everybody has got to help the law of course. That's rather a threadbare platitude and I know that it isn't entirely consoling, but all the same it is true, and as you have done it, I'm going to take advantage of it."

"I was afraid you might." Gardiner pulled a wry face.

"If I do, that won't be your fault; and I won't bring you into it. All I shall do is to say that I am a detective sent up at the request of the Coroner to make formal investigations. I shall say that in view of the suddenness of the death, the Coroner feels that there must be an inquest, and that therefore enquiries must be made, despite the fact that I understand that Cargate's own doctor is quite willing to sign almost any certificate. Then I shall begin to make those enquiries. All that I shall suppress is that I come from Scotland Yard and I shall apparently do my work superficially in rather a formal, almost stupid manner, so that everyone, *everyone,* will think that I am a conscientious but unimaginative sort of chap, fitted only to carry out routine work. I shall get more told to me in that way, and I want you to treat me as if I were such a person and not let anyone know who I really am."

"I shall keep quiet. In fact I probably shall not see anyone who is concerned, but I don't think that you will get away with it."

"Why not?" Fenby looked a little hurt and then unexpectedly grinned. "After all, I am pretty stupid."

"You may be—though I doubt it. But anyone with as much intelligence as—let us say—the gardener will inevitably smell a rat. I should imagine that Miss Knox Forster must do so, and in the absence of anybody else, she's rather in control down there."

"Until Ley comes down. I have warned him by the way not to talk—a feat which he may find difficult. But, if necessary, I shall have to take Miss Knox Forster into my confidence."

"You'll find her a very useful ally."

"Shall I? That's worth knowing, but I shall see how things go before I take her at all into my confidence. Meanwhile can you tell me anything about any of the staff who have stayed on. I understand that Cargate only came to live at Scotney End Hall quite recently. Also I should like to know more about the vicar."

"Cargate has only been there since the spring. I don't remember the exact date. How long Miss Knox Forster has been in his employment I don't know. Raikes, I have an impression, for some time, but the housemaids and so on are all new. The gardener is the only local man."

"Interesting; but how do you know all this as you weren't his doctor?"

"This is a country district and one's business is not one's own. Every action of a man in Cargate's position would obviously be discussed at length, if not always with truth, and as I go on my rounds, they try to gossip to me in every cottage. I honestly do my best to stop them, not so much because it bores or embarrasses me, as because I have not got the time to waste. Nevertheless I am bound to get some of it, especially when there is a grievance, which was exactly what Scotney End had got. Cargate, you see, employed as few people locally as he could, and it made a considerable difference to the parish. They did not mind when it was somebody well established in Cargate's household such as Raikes, but they did object to newly engaged cooks and housemaids. Hence their knowledge, forced upon me, and a rather nasty feeling in the village."

Fenby sighed. If everyone's hand in Scotney End had been against Cargate, it broadened the field of his search and at the same time it might mean that everyone would rather shield the murderer than otherwise.

"'A considerable difference to the parish'," he repeated. "That brings us back to the vicar."

"A very old friend of mine. The soul of honour who never did a dirty thing in his life and to whom everyone in Scotney End, everyone who really belonged there, that is, was devoted, and to all of whom he in his turn was genuinely attached."

"So much so that he might be prepared to go to great lengths to help them?"

"Ridiculous. Of course I see what you mean, but you don't know Yockleton."

"I don't, and really so far only the vaguest ideas are in my mind. All the same it seems to me that paradoxically one can only connect him with it if he is an absolutely first-class man, prepared to sacrifice himself for the benefit of others."

"He is all that, but all the same—"

"Oh! I agree. It's very far-fetched and I don't really mean it. Besides, in any case, a bad tenant is better than none at all, and big houses are very hard to let these days."

"Scotney End Hall isn't so vast as that, and I must admit that it has always been said that it is one of the few houses for which there would always be a purchaser or an occupant

of some sort. The old squire always said that he could have
let it at any moment and he often talked of doing so. But
every time that it came to the point he couldn't bear, hard
up though he was, to contemplate anyone else living there,
even for a moment. Certainly when he died, his executors
had no difficulty in selling it at once. I heard a rumour
that they were rather sorry about it. The family's recovered
some of its money and I shouldn't be at all surprised if they
bought it back now. There'll be great rejoicings in Scotney
End if they do. But all the same, don't get ideas into your
head about Yockleton."

Fenby laughed and admitted that any ideas at all were pre-
mature. Nevertheless it did seem to him that so far Cargate's
death was proving too exclusively an unmixed benefit.

"Probably," he thought to himself, "I shall end by deciding
to suspect only the people who are injured by it. I must say
that I hope it won't come to that. A purely altruistic murder
would be the devil to solve. All the same I shall have to talk
rather earnestly to the Reverend Mr. Yockleton."

Had Fenby but known it, the subject of Cargate's death
was at that moment keeping the vicar of Scotney End, a man
who usually went to bed very early, sitting up in his study at
an hour that he regarded as incredibly late.

As yet, of course, no word of Fenby had reached him.
There had been talk of a Coroner, he understood, and his
friend, Dr. Gardiner, had, he heard, strangely impounded
the snuffbox, that beautiful piece of craftsmanship which
he had always longed to examine more at his leisure, and
which indeed he had had a brief chance to examine only
the morning before, but these, so the vicar was told by Miss
Knox Forster, were normal activities.

Therefore it was not such things that were worrying him

but the fight with his own conscience. For, for the first time in his life, he was glad of the death of a man, violently and unrestrainedly glad, and equally violently and unrestrainedly ashamed of being so delighted. Until the point was settled so that either he had ceased indecently to rejoice, or alternatively had come to an honest conclusion that it was not wicked to do so, there would be no sleep for him.

From the very first moment when he had met Cargate he had felt that an evil influence had come into his life, or rather, and it mattered more to him, into the life of everyone in his parish. It was not that Cargate was rich; Yockleton was far beyond the cant of thinking that rich men must necessarily be bad or that they must necessarily have acquired their riches by devious means when in fact he did not know how they had been obtained. His complaint was not even that Cargate used his riches badly. In fact, Yockleton saw no harm in most of the things on which Cargate spent his money, which apparently consisted on the one hand of paying too much to those who did anything for him, and on the other, forming collections of objects varying from snuffboxes to postage stamps. There could be no objection to any of this, but there was harm, to Yockleton's mind, in the open way in which Cargate flaunted and worshipped his wealth.

Next came the question of religion. Yockleton was not a narrow-minded man and he was prepared to believe, though with difficulty, that there could be good in those who neglected to pay even a formal lip service to the Church of England or any other form of Christian worship. It would have been hard for him to have as his principal parishioner one who was not a member of his flock, but it would not have produced the intensity of feeling which he had if Cargate had not so openly sneered at religion of all sorts. When, for instance, Cargate, with a very real interest in the subject, had wanted to pull down the vestry or break open two tombs, simply in order to find out if there were really as he believed the remains of something, and Yockleton had never quite found out what, underneath, he had been genuinely hurt and shocked; and Cargate, with whom archaeology was occasionally an overmastering passion, had been almost equally shocked at his refusal.

Then there had been differences of opinion about employment in the parish, for to Yockleton the first duty of the man who lived at Scotney End Hall was to see to the welfare of the inhabitants of Scotney End. As an idea it might have been dubbed not unfairly as old-fashioned, out-moded relic of squire-archy, but it was generally held by the vicar as a duty, and to his mind people ought in no circumstances ever to neglect their duties. Whereas Cargate regarded the village people as surly, unfriendly, incompetent, and wished so far as possible to ignore their very existence. The only thing that he could see in their favour was that they seemed to want, in their turn, to ignore him. Unfortunately that was a delusion.

The state of affairs then, when on the morning of Thursday, July 12th, Yockleton had gone up in a last desperate effort to bring Cargate round to his way of thinking, had been anything but propitious. Even Yockleton himself had known really that his visit could serve no useful purpose, but he had felt that he ought to try. His actual excuse was the return to Scotney End of a possible under-gardener, known locally as Scottish Hardy.

It should be explained that in the village the Hardys were so numerous and so invariably christened William, that they were usually distinguished by adding their occupation or abode—both Hardy the Hedger and Hardy Except were well-recognized descriptions, the latter living in a row of cottages built by a pious man who had caused to be inscribed along their entire front: "Except the Lord build the house, they labour in vain who build it."

Scottish Hardy, however, had not found work in the village. He had—and the village was inclined to regard the action as in doubtful taste—joined the army as an accidental result, due to an adventurous disposition, of going up to London to see the Cup Final, which incidentally he never reached. There were several rather confused stages before he reached the recruiting office, but even so he had never intended to do anything more exotic than join the battalion of his own county, but an excessive emphasis on the name of the village in which he lived had resulted in the authorities, who in any case found his East Anglian speech hard to follow, placing him in what they understood was his local battalion, the Royal Scots Fusiliers.

Now, after a period of reasonably blameless and quite undistinguished service, followed by a period at a vocational training centre, he found himself unemployed and alleged to be trained as a gardener. Even Yockleton felt a little doubtful as to how exhaustive was the training which had been crammed into the last few weeks or months of his service.

But he had no doubt that Cargate, who wanted several gardeners, ought to give Scottish Hardy a trial and a certain amount of additional training. Cargate, however, did not see it in the very least.

"What I need are competent people who know their jobs," was the opinion that he expressed. "I am neither capable nor willing to teach people what they ought to know before I employ them."

"But you have got a man he would work under."

"And a fat lot he knows, so far as I can see."

"But he's been here for years and years!"

"And learned nothing the whole time."

Yockleton was nothing if not persevering. "Scottish Hardy has had *some* training, you know."

"You don't call an army vocational centre *training*, do you? Just a smattering of knowledge is all they give them, so that they can impose themselves upon a trusting public."

"I really think that they do more for them than that. I'm only suggesting that you give him a trial. If he doesn't prove to be any good, well, then it's a different matter, but I'm sure he will. For one thing he's a disciplined man and so he'll be easy to teach."

But Cargate had laughed openly at that suggestion.

"They don't stay in the army long enough to get discipline as a second nature, and directly they come out, they react at once and become quite impossible. All they remember or ever learn in the army is how to dodge work, and they are pretty good at doing that."

"I do not agree with you. Not for a moment." The vicar was on the verge of losing his temper. "Besides, I can't help being aware of the fact that accommodation for anyone who does not belong here is very difficult to get. Now Scottish Hardy's family live just by the post-office—"

"I am aware—very well aware—of the difficulties placed in my way in this village and I think," he looked significantly at Yockleton, "that I know to whom I am entitled to attribute the presence of those impediments."

"Are you suggesting—?"

"I am." Cargate did not believe it for a moment but he wanted to be done with the vicar's interferences once and for all. "I'm not quite such a fool as you appear to think that I am, and when I find organized obstruction amongst a lot of uneducated peasants who would be quite unable for themselves to think of any practical method of expressing the dislike with which they honour me, and quite unable to carry it out if they did, I look round to see who can be the organizer, and when I find only one person present who can possibly have sufficient intelligence to devise the scheme, well, I put two and two together."

"Of course if you start from a series of utterly false premises, it is possible to build up a logical structure and arrive at results which are grotesquely absurd—"

"I always start from known facts. I must apparently remind you that you yourself mentioned that difficulties were being put in my way."

"They certainly are. But they arise not from me, though I will admit that there are many aspects of your conduct which make the carrying out of my duties difficult. I had hoped to discuss some of those with you to-day, but in the mood in which we both are, that would be impossible."

"Quite. Suppose then that this interview ceases? Once and for all."

"Those difficulties arise," Yockleton went on, ignoring the interruption and determined to go on with what he felt it was his duty to say, "from the spontaneous action and unanimous opinion of everyone in Scotney End—"

"And you really pretend that that opinion has not been carefully coached? Would it surprise you to know that I have proof of that?"

"It would indeed."

"Very well then, I shall give it to you." Cargate turned to ring the bell and then stopped. "On the whole," he said, "I think that I shall get it myself. It's a very simple proof but I forget exactly where I put it."

In a few minutes he was back again in the room and striding indignantly to the fireplace where he angrily pulled the bell.

"That clock in the hall is slow again, Raikes," he said when the butler appeared. "It is now 11.17 and it points to 11.15. I told you yesterday to have it put right."

"The man from Great Barwick, sir, has not yet—"

"I told you to have it put right. Now, Mr. Yockleton, it may surprise you to know that I take in your parish—" Cargate broke off suddenly. "I see you are looking at my snuffbox, a beautiful thing, is it not? It belonged to one of the Prince Regent's friends who, like myself, took an occasional pinch. I expect he took it more often than the once every other day that I permit myself. That is his monogram worked round that central emerald. By the way, Mr. Yockleton, that emerald was there this morning when I handed it to Raikes to clean out some fragments that lingered in it of stale snuff. It's very strange that it should be missing just after you have been looking at it. However, to return to your parish magazine. This article of yours on 'The Duty of Mutual Help' in a small community such as you rightly observe, Scotney End is, would seem—"

"Did you suggest just now," Yockleton had taken almost a quarter of a minute to recover from the shock, "that I had stolen a jewel of yours?"

"It was loose before and easily prised out of its setting with a little force. But one thing at a time. This article as I was saying points directly at me and actively encourages everyone in Scotney End to take the attitude that I feel is so very deplorable."

"Stop. I refuse to listen to a word more until you remove the accusation that you have made."

"About the emerald? I may be wrong. It only seemed to me a very peculiar coincidence. If you really want to disprove it, perhaps you wouldn't object to being searched?"

"Really, Mr. Cargate! May I remind you that I am the vicar of this parish?"

"Ah! I thought that the idea of being searched would not appeal to you. It's quite a valuable emerald."

Yockleton thought a minute. It was a ridiculous and obviously trumped-up charge. Probably that was the reason why Cargate had himself gone to get the parish magazine, since otherwise he would not have been left by himself in the library of Scotney End Hall. Probably too the suggestion that he should be searched contained a trick too. The vicar was quite astute and he foresaw what might well happen.

"I won't be searched by you," he answered, "because you would be certain to plant the thing on me, if you haven't already done so."

"Quite experienced, I see," Cargate remarked pleasantly. Then, changing suddenly from the light tone which he had been adopting, he went on without worrying to veil his contemptuous anger. "In a few minutes I am going to show you a wasps' nest; on the table there, quite close to my snuffbox, is a bottle containing potassium cyanide. To-night the one rather incompetent gardener whom I have is going to use the contents of that bottle to destroy those pestilential insects. From where that wasps' nest is we shall be able to get a view, a distant view I am glad to say, of the village of Scotney End. I hope that its inhabitants will not become as troublesome to me as those of the hole in the ground by which we shall be standing, for I am as interested in the one as in the other, and I shall find it equally easy to deal with either."

"Really, sir! Your lack of humanity!"

"Is only equalled by my knowledge of how to deal competently with human beings. Even when they are queen wasps who buzz round and annoy me with their silly noise and sillier writings and even threaten to sting if they knew but how. Indeed, I have taken a fancy to show you this nest."

"I have no desire to see it."

"Perhaps not, but I think that it would be as well if you did. When we get there I shall relieve you of the emerald and at the same time explain to you how it could have been found in your possession. A simple trick, Mr. Yockleton; perhaps in view of your reputation and profession, it might not have been successful, but one which can easily be repeated if there is necessity on a more elaborate and convincing scale. Now, allow me to show you this wasps' nest and, on the way, the outside of the front door. There will be no need for you to see the inside again. This way please. Ah! Miss Knox Forster," he continued as he caught sight of his secretary in the hall, "the vicar is inclined to be angry with me, as you have no doubt observed from the rather mottled condition of his face. I have been so unfortunate as to incur his displeasure by refusing to employ an army protégé of his of whom I have heard no good accounts. However, I am going to soothe him down by showing him our wasps' nest. It won't be there any more after to-day."

"Now I wonder just what all that was about," Joan Knox Forster said to herself as the front door closed behind them, "though I think that I can guess. What is it, Raikes?"

"About the clock, Miss. I've sent for the man to come but they don't seem to hurry in these parts, and Mr. Cargate's going on something shocking about it, if you will excuse me saying so, and I don't rightly know what to do. I don't seem to be able to do anything right to-day."

"Is your own watch reliable?"

"Very fairly so, Miss."

"Then set the clock morning and evening by it until the man comes. And go on doing it, because it will probably be just as bad after he has gone as it is now."

Raikes sighed. It was certainly a simple way out which had even occurred to him, but his life was getting complicated by having to remember so many little trifles of that sort. If only his employer would occasionally make allowances! He didn't think that he could stick it much longer.

• ● ● ● •

"Therefore at 11.15 the Reverend Mr. Yockleton was alone in the library of Scotney End Hall and both the snuffbox and the poison were available. Moreover he had just been most unjustifiably attacked, and was feeling outraged and indignant. Then again, round about 11.30 the library was empty for perhaps eight minutes while Mr. Cargate persisted in walking with Mr. Yockleton to the banks of the moat which once completely surrounded the Hall and still exists on three sides of the house. There he showed the protesting vicar a hole in the ground in a sunny patch between the shade of two elm trees and pointed out to him the insects that were continually making their way to and from it. Then, I understand, with a parting insult, he turned on his heel and made his way back to the house.

"During that time, perhaps, as I have said, eight minutes, there were two people who were in and about the hall, from which I must remind you, the library could be entered. They were Miss Joan Knox Forster and Alfred Raikes. You will hear that they had a few minutes' conversation and that then both of them went about their duties, Raikes to lay the table and attend to the silver in the dining-room, while Miss Knox Forster happened to be passing to and fro putting fresh flowers about the house. The statements which those two persons have made as to the exact movements of themselves and of the other do not entirely agree but—I wish to be absolutely fair—you may come to the conclusion that neither of them had any reason to take any very particular notice of what was happening and therefore it is natural that there should be some difference of opinion, or you may take a contrary view and consider that they should be more consistent. For the present I only wish to point out that those eight minutes must be noted.

"For the moment I will leave that matter where it stands and I will also pass over for the present the long period of time to which I have referred, though I shall return to it, and I shall next call to your attention the third short period which occurred in the afternoon of this same day at, as I have stated, about 3.30 p.m. I am afraid that I must necessarily involve you in some discussion on the subject of philately, a term which, as you know, means, in more simple language, the collecting of postage stamps.

"I need hardly tell you" (as in the case of all people who use that phrase, Blayton immediately proceeded to do so) "that whereas stamp collecting can be a very simple matter when it is carried out by the young—and I should be on the whole surprised to hear that none of you, members of the jury, indulged in the insidious pastime in your youth—when it infects, if I may use the term, those of mature years, it develops complications thus resembling those many childish complaints, infectious diseases and so forth, which have little effect on those of tender years but which are very serious when contracted by adults."

Blayton smiled cheerfully at the jury at what he considered a very happy metaphor in a light vein and then recollecting, rather belatedly, that it was not impossible that some of his hearers might still be stamp collectors who might not like to have it implied that they were suffering from a form of mental measles or mumps, he went on hurriedly: "Not of course that there are not very great benefits to be derived from a hobby which has obtained the patronage even of royalty. I only mean to imply that it is in its higher branches a very highly elaborate and technical hobby. I understand that the complete philatelist must be fully cognizant of the processes of papermaking and printing as well as of perforating and water-marking the paper used. He must know all about type, printer's ink, 'make ready', laid and wove papers, grilles, photogravure, line-engraving, and he must be thoroughly well acquainted with the methods of detecting forgeries of all kinds, alterations even in the postmark, and of observing the most minute repairs. When I add that the philatelist will incidentally acquire an addition to his knowledge of history and geography, I shall, I am sure, have convinced you that the hobby is a learned one.

"Even we, I am afraid, my lord, shall have to acquire some knowledge on the matter."

"Assuming, Mr. Blayton, that we do not already possess it." Mr. Justice Smith saw no reason why he should be selected as the representative of ignorance, even though, as a fact, he did not himself collect stamps. Still, for all Blayton knew, he might.

"Quite, my lord. But I fear that it is too much to hope that in addition to yourself, all the counsel concerned, and all the jury are stamp collectors."

"Probably, but you never can tell, Mr. Blayton. However,

proceed. You were saying that there were certain matters of which we should have—I think you said 'to acquire some knowledge'."

"Exactly, my lord. We shall have to hear something of mixed perforations, of accents inserted by hand, of a missing fraction bar, of the phrase '*se tenant*', for, members of the jury, whether his lordship or I are stamp collectors is immaterial. What matters is that Henry Cargate was, and a very advanced one too, with a magnificent collection, and that on the afternoon of July 12th, from 2.30 to 3.45 he was visited by Andrew Macpherson, a dealer in rare stamps, who for once and as a special favour to an important client, left his offices in the Strand and proceeded to Scotney End.

"What happened there is this…"

Andrew Macpherson disliked the railway journey to Larkingfield very much, and he grudged intensely the time spent in going there. For almost no other client would he ever have considered leaving his office, let alone going out of London.

But Cargate was a very exceptional client for a variety of reasons. In the first place he spent a great deal of money. In the second place, or so he said, owing to ill-health he found it inconvenient to be in London very often, and thirdly Macpherson himself was a little unhappy about certain aspects of Cargate's philatelic habits. If what he suspected was true, Cargate was definitely a menace to the stamp trade.

The second point would normally have presented very little difficulty. Macpherson had many clients, valuable and trusted clients, whom he had infrequently or even never seen. He sent them portions of his stock on approval, or offered them parcels which he had bought at auction or privately if he happened to know that they were likely to be of interest to them. Indeed his business depended to some extent on throwing the right fly over each collector without ever forcing anything, or being in danger for a moment of being a nuisance. On the principle of the greatest mutual trust and interest, it worked very well and Macpherson prided himself on taking a very genuine interest in the collections of quite a number of people.

But it had to be a matter of mutual trust. He had, practically speaking, to guarantee the genuineness in every detail of every stamp that he sold, and he had, on the other hand, to entrust his stock to the hands of a great many people whom he really only knew slightly. If they accidentally damaged them, he had to rely on their honesty to say so. If an item was sent out by mistake unpriced, or only priced in pencil, he had to trust them not to remove it or rub out the price, and in either case say nothing about it. Finally he had to take the risk that they would not take his good specimens and substitute damaged ones or, what was worse, replace valuable varieties with quite common ones. It was all a trifle hazardous because with a stock of hundreds of thousands of stamps, he could not keep track of every one, nor if he did could he be certain whether to blame the collector who had the book last or the one before that. The damage might have been done weeks before.

It is probable that there is no body of men who have a higher sense of honour than stamp dealers. To put it at the lowest, it is absolutely essential to them since stamp collecting is an absolutely artificial trade, and if there is one thing which may kill it for ever, it would be the discovery of a large number of forgeries. There are indeed certain countries whose stamps have been imitated extensively, and they are collected only by a very few people. Of all this the stamp dealer is well aware and for that reason is always on the look-out to help the public.

To the collector the restraint is less present, but the temptation to forge, if not to steal, is less. To manufacture bogus stamps to put into your collection gives no more satisfaction than cheating at patience; to do it to make money, apart from considerations of honesty is highly dangerous because it is so extremely difficult.

In all his years of experience—and he had entered his father's business as a boy when the stamp trade was just beginning to boom at the end of the nineteenth century—Macpherson had never known more than the most trivial and petty pieces of dishonesty until he began to have dealings with Cargate, and even then he only suspected without quite having proof.

Cargate, like all advanced collectors, made no attempt to obtain the stamps of every country. He confined himself to two groups, first the British West Indies and secondly the issues of Great Britain including British stamps overprinted for use elsewhere. It may, to those who preserve their sanity and avoid stamps carefully, sound a severe restriction, but those who have allowed themselves to be infected by the virus of a hobby which once it is allowed to get into the blood is never wholly eradicated, will know that actually it is a very extensive—and expensive—field.

It was over the question of some stamps of the Bahamas that Macpherson had first begun to get worried. Cargate had on that occasion come to him and said that he had some duplicates of which he would like to get rid. With that he had opened a small leather-bound book specially fitted for carrying loose stamps and had displayed the contents.

Macpherson could remember still the surprise with which he had observed what was there. At that time Cargate had been a fairly new client and he had no idea that he had a collection at all out of the way.

"This is pretty good stuff. These old Bahamas in mint condition are pretty scarce. Are they all without watermark or are any of them Crown C. C.?"

"You can tell from the colour. You don't get that lavender grey in the later ones."

"Quite. But that doesn't apply to the pennies, or, for that matter, to the fourpenny dull rose." Macpherson was a good-tempered man but he disliked being snubbed as much as anyone else; besides, he probably knew more about the tricky first issues of Bahamas than anyone else. To cover up his annoyance he bent over the stamps and exclaimed: "That fourpenny and sixpenny are magnificent. They're one of the good perforations too."

"Do you really think that you can tell perforations at a glance?" There seemed to be a sneer in the question.

"Those aren't the perf. fourteen to sixteen, which, though they are nice enough, aren't quite the best. Nor do I think they are perf. thirteen. Even so there are two choices left."

"As a matter of fact they are the compound perforation. Eleven and a half or twelve with eleven."

"The devil they are! Mint! And duplicates! It seems too good to be true."

"They've been in my family for a long while. I had a great-uncle who was out there and he, fortunately for me, brought a good many things back. It seems a pity not to let those that I don't want get in circulation."

"Personally I should want to keep all that I ever got of these. But before buying them I should want to measure all these perforations very carefully. The differences aren't very easy to tell."

"I do not find it so hard. In fact I will tell you quite frankly that if you disagree with me I shall continue to prefer my own opinion."

"I may have to stick to mine all the same. Do you mind waiting a minute, sir? I'd like to get a new instrument which has just come on the market."

"Very well then. But don't be long, I haven't got much time to spare." Cargate had sat in the inner office of the shop impatiently drumming his fingers on the table. He might know all about compound perforations, but what this new invention was he had no idea. Still less could he have imagined that years later the question was to be faintly referred to in a law court and that a painstaking barrister was to have to explain that "Perf. 14" meant that there were fourteen perforation holes cut in a length of two centimetres, or that "compound perf." meant that the stamp was perforated partially on one gauge and partially on another.

However, at the time he was only interested in what Macpherson had just brought into the office. It appeared to be a combination of a lamp and magnifying glass or even telescope, and down it Macpherson was peering intently with a face growing rapidly graver.

"Are you quite sure these have never been in any other hands than your great-uncle's and your own?"

"Quite. Why?"

"Then I'm afraid that somebody imposed on your great-uncle."

"I've always understood that he bought them from the post-office himself."

"Have you ever used one of these ultra-ray lamps, sir?"

"No."

"Then perhaps you would like to look down it now. Just put your eye there."

Cargate looked, and there was no doubt that there was genuine amazement on his face. The dull rose stamp with the young Queen's head surrounded by a crown seemed to fall into two pieces. The stones of the pearl necklace which she was represented as wearing seemed distinctly and unfortunately printed on quite a separate piece of paper to that on which the words "fourpence" were. Without comment Macpherson removed the stamp and substituted the lavender-grey sixpenny value to which he had referred before. It looked, under the lamp, as if it were composed of six different pieces of paper of which the one at the top bearing the word "Bahamas" now appeared to be a totally different colour.

"Part of the sixpenny violet of the later issue, I should think—and a pen-cancelled specimen at that, judging by the smear of ink by the 'H'—faded gradually in the sun and then coloured carefully the right shade. I should destroy those stamps if I were you, sir."

"I shall, I think." Cargate had looked thoroughly uneasy. "I can't think how or why it was done, but it's a marvellous piece of work. Take them away from that machine and you would never spot the joins."

"Never. It's a wonderful machine too."

"It is." Cargate looked at it angrily. "I wish it hadn't been invented. It seems to me to be definitely a case of where ignorance is bliss."

On the whole Cargate had carried it off so well—he had even retained his air of contemptuous disdain—that at the time Macpherson had been quite unable to believe, although of course the idea occurred to him at once, that the repairs had been carried out by Cargate himself. To offer for sale as a genuine stamp one composed of four or five pieces of which only some were ever part of the stamp the whole was supposed to be, with the perforations tampered with so as to represent the scarcest variety, was undoubtedly dishonest if it had been done consciously. But had it? Macpherson, incapable of such a thing himself, was inclined to give Cargate the benefit of the doubt. As to the great-uncle who was alleged to have brought them home, either he had amused himself by making up these fraudulent works of art just for the fun of doing so and without intent to part with them, or Cargate was wrong, and he had not bought them from the post-office in the Bahamas, but in this country, and from some dishonest person.

The impression of honesty was on the whole increased when Cargate came in some months later and asked him if he would test the genuineness by means of his lamp of a pair of stamps which he had been offered, though at a rather high price. Macpherson professed himself delighted, but then added:

"You really ought to get one of these lamps, sir. They don't cost a very great deal. It's well worth the while of any serious collector."

"If you don't want to let me use it—"

"But by all means, sir, by all means. Pleased to do a little thing like that for a less good customer than yourself. What are the stamps this time, sir? I hope that I shan't have bad news for you a second time."

On this occasion the stamps proved to be a pair of British green and red twopenny stamps of the last type of the Victorian issues, both of which were overprinted "British Protectorate Oil Rivers" and in addition both were surcharged with the words "One Shilling" with a bar underneath. But while one of the surcharges was in violet, one was in black.

"You certainly do bring me scarce things to look at. The black surcharge is catalogued a hundred and twenty pounds by itself and *se tenant* with the violet one, it must be unique. I do hope all's well."

Once more the lamp came into play, and once more there was to be disappointment. There was no doubt that the colour of the black surcharge was originally the same as that of the violet one. Traces of the old colour and the chemical used to alter the shade were still visible.

"I am afraid that they are only a pair in the black ink. Rare enough even so, but nothing like what they appear to be. I'm beginning to have doubts about the genuineness of the whole surcharge too." Macpherson fell to examining the pair once more.

"It doesn't matter," Cargate broke out, "I shan't be buying it. Dishonest lot you stamp dealers are."

Macpherson drew up his tall, rather gaunt frame to its full height and shook his grey hair violently.

"No, on the whole definitely not. And I must ask you not to say such things again."

"With those things in front of you?"

"There may be an occasional wrong 'un in the trade. What trade hasn't got one or two? But if we can find him out, we out him pretty quickly. Who supplied you with this?"

"Never you mind."

Macpherson pressed for the information as much as he could, but it was useless. Cargate absolutely refused to give the name which, if Macpherson had been a better judge of character or had known Cargate more intimately, he would have realized in itself was suspicious, for normally Cargate was prepared to betray anyone. As it was the stamp dealer soon gave it up.

"Though if I knew who it was, I'd murder him," he muttered to himself, inwardly adding: "and if I was quite sure that it was you—" But outwardly he said no more.

Nevertheless from that time onward Macpherson had always kept a very wary eye open when he was dealing with

Cargate. For that matter the freemasonry amongst the dealers practically obliged him to drop a guarded hint or two to his fellow dealers. But for a long while he had no cause to complain. At first it had surprised him that Cargate still came to his shop; but when he persisted the surprise wore off. On the whole it seemed to augur well for Cargate's innocence, though it was undoubtedly true that Macpherson had one of the best, if not the best, stock of those countries in which Cargate was interested. Also Cargate, like all other collectors, did not confine himself to one dealer.

But beyond those two incidents Macpherson had never had any reason to suspect Cargate's honesty, a ridiculous idea anyhow to hold of a man so obviously wealthy, until the day when Macpherson, much protesting, was induced to go down to Scotney End Hall.

"Nevertheless," Fenby said, "you went down to Larking-field."

It was some days after he had started his investigation at Scotney End. Indeed he had come up from there to see Macpherson and he would be going down there again very soon in all probability.

"I did," Macpherson answered. "I didn't want to, but Cargate was always difficult and tried to make me come to him. On the whole it was worth my while to do so, and also on this occasion he had made some imputations about some stamps which I had sent to him on approval which had to be cleared up by a personal interview."

"You did let part of your stock be in his hands, despite your doubts as to his honesty?"

"Before that afternoon when I went to Scotney End, there were only two occasions when I had any doubt about him. One might have been a case where he, or his uncle, had been imposed upon. The other was when he asked my opinion about some stamps which he said he was thinking of buying. I was pretty sure that the surcharges of both were wholly bogus. In other words that two stamps worth a few shillings each had been turned into a pair, one of which would be catalogued seven pounds and one a hundred and twenty and worth, as a pair, more than that. But I had no reason to think that he was responsible for either of them."

"Yet you went round to Ley as his executor and told him that he ought not to try to sell Cargate's collection without having it very carefully examined first?"

"Yes."

"Just exactly why?"

"I had seen his St. Vincents in the interval."

"What was wrong with them?"

"A great many of them are perfectly all right. In fact I've sold many of them to him myself. But scattered amongst them are things that I believe are forgeries. So I think that they all ought to be examined."

"I see. Can you, without being too technical, give me an idea of what may be wrong. I mean if they are palpable forgeries, it does not matter. And if they were hard to notice, I don't see how you know. I gather you did not have a long examination."

"No. He was out of the room for quite a short while, but they happen to be stamps of which I know a good deal. The really good old St. Vincent stamps, especially well-centred copies with good colour and which have not had their perforations damaged or played about with, are all scarce."

"How scarce? I mean I have heard that a stamp has fetched about five thousand pounds."

"We aren't dealing with the Post Office Mauritius or the

British Guiana one cent black on magenta. No, these St. Vincents are worth anything up to a hundred pounds, but the best of them perhaps, though others are catalogued just as highly, are some provisionals issued in 1880 and 1881; especially the halfpenny on half of the sixpenny in pair, one having a fraction bar to the figure ½ and one having it missing. Gibbons, though for what reason they select these stamps only and not many others, I do not know, deliberately do not illustrate the surcharges correctly. In fact they say so. But I know them when I see them and a good many other things about them too, and Cargate's, I could see at a glance, did not pass muster in all cases, but they would have been accepted by a great many people."

"I see. That seems a reason for warning Ley. But what was Cargate's object? I mean why consciously put forged stamps in your own collection?"

"One of two things. Either he was in touch with someone who was a forger—in which case he himself was the dupe; or he wanted to show off—he was that sort of man—and make the collection look better than it was."

"But he could have bought the genuine ones? He was pretty rich, I understand."

"No one, though I would not like to confess it too openly, is rich enough to buy all the stamps that he wants. I think it was vanity on his part; but whether he did it or not they are, believe me, pretty dangerous forgeries. Not to me, or to any one of a dozen other people in London, and perhaps as many more elsewhere, but nearly everyone else would be deceived. Even some experts might pass them, which is why I want those stamps destroyed."

Fenby could not help wondering if it also provided a reason for why Macpherson wanted Cargate destroyed, that is, if Macpherson really thought that Cargate was the forger. Therefore he went on to say meditatively:

"I suppose you would like to know who the forger is."

"I certainly would, and I suppose that forgery being a crime you would help me to find out."

"We should have to have something more definite on which to work, but if somebody, not knowing that Cargate has died, sends along a selection, I'll promise to get in touch with you."

"I should be grateful, but I don't think anyone will. I think Cargate did it himself."

"But you said just now, as I understood it, that you were in fact trusting him? No, that was before you saw these St. Vincent stamps. But even then you weren't sure."

"It was what happened that afternoon after he came back into the room which convinced me."

"I see. Perhaps you had better give me an account of what happened." It was in fact exactly what Fenby had come to find out, but he far preferred reaching it by indirect methods, and the fact that Macpherson had been at pains to find out from Miss Knox Forster who was Cargate's executor and give him a warning as to the disposal of the collection, had been a convenient chance which had made his appearance in Macpherson's office more natural.

"My orders were," Macpherson accentuated the word "orders" with a slight sarcastic bitterness, "to call on him at 2.30 p.m. For that purpose I was to be picked up at the inn in Larkingfield at quarter past two. You see he made it quite clear that I was not good enough to have lunch with him and I think that I had equally implied that I would not lunch in the servants' hall. However, at 2.30 I arrived and was shown in to him."

"Into the library?"

"I suppose so. On the left of the hall as you come in."

"Quite. Go on."

"He was looking at these St. Vincent stamps which I mentioned to you and he immediately began to tell me what a wonderful collection of them he had. In fact he told me that I was never likely to see such a remarkably fine lot of them again, and to imply that he was conferring a great favour by letting me see them. Actually I have had many lots quite as good through my hands, but his were undoubtedly very fine. There was no denying that. Or rather they would have been if they had been what they purported to be."

"But they weren't?"

"They were not. I suppose that Cargate's tone and manner ruffled me and that therefore I was critical." Macpherson ran his hand through his grey hair so that it certainly looked literally ruffled while he himself seemed to get quite irritable at the very thought. "Anyhow, I looked at them carefully and I suppose my expression gave me away."

Fenby, looking at the dealer, thought that in all probability his face was often far more expressive than he knew. However, that was not a point which he wanted to stress, so he brought the conversation back to the point.

"You saw at once that some of them were forged?"

"One or two of them. At least I very strongly suspected it and I made a mistake. I at once asked him where he had got one particular stamp from. 'Not from you,' was his answer. 'I hope not,' I said. At that he got thoroughly cross and asked what I was implying. I told him that I guaranteed the genuineness of everything I sold and that I would not be sure of that particular copy. It was the pair of halfpenny on sixpence which I have already mentioned to you. On that he turned thoroughly nasty and said that in future he would not show me things that were too good for me to look at. If you come to think of it it would have been more reasonable if he had said that he would never have any more dealings with me again, but he knew quite well that that would be cutting off his own nose to spite his face, because I was certain to get hold of what he wanted, so he confined himself to being rude and he ended by saying that I was in no position to talk because I was in the habit of submitting very peculiar items in my own approval books. That, of course, I indignantly denied. It was in fact the point I had come down to discuss with him. You remember I said something of it?"

"Yes. And was this also concerned with the stamps of St. Vincent?"

"No. It happened to be Ireland this time. There isn't anything very frightfully special there, but some of the no-accent varieties are fairly good."

Fenby groaned.

"Must I understand about them too?"

"It's quite easy. Some of them have the word 'Saorstát' on them. It means, I think, 'Free State', and there ought to be an accent on the second 'á', but here and there it's missing. On the ten shilling it's a fairly good stamp, and it was about a block of four, one with the accent missing, that he had made his dirty insinuations." Macpherson got quite heated as he recalled the incident.

"He accused me, if you please," he went on, "of having removed the accent from the face of one of them and of having attempted to do the same to the back. Now that would be a foolish trick because the pressure of the printing would always leave a mark, a ridge so to speak, where the stamping had pushed the paper out, and I don't believe that you could remove it. Besides, I do not do that sort of thing anyhow. All the same I will admit that it was a very unpleasant accusation to have made to one, because even the rumour of it, if it were spread about to a really considerable extent, would damage my business very seriously. You can easily see that if people did not trust me, they would only buy common things from me since they could be certain of them, it not being worth while to spend several hours turning a stamp worth sixpence into a stamp worth ninepence. But nobody would rely on me to sell them anything decent, if you understand what I mean."

"I quite see. But what evidence did Cargate bring as to this accusation?"

"A block of four stamps on one of which in fact an attempt had been made to remove this accent."

"Which he had with him?"

"Which were stuck into my approval book. But not by me. Or by any of my assistants. They wouldn't be such fools as to do it on purpose. They might, I suppose, have stolen the genuine ones and put in this manufactured variety, but I do not believe it. They have all been with me at least five years and I have never known anything of the sort happen before. But, to go back, Cargate told me of this block and I, of course, at once said that I didn't believe him, and asked him to show it to me. 'I certainly shall,' was his answer, 'in fact I have every intention of doing so. I meant to have the book handy but you arrived a few minutes early, so I must just get it out of my safe.' With that he left the room and I, as I told you, took a further look at the St. Vincents on his writing-table. Perhaps that was a mistake because it led to even further unpleasantness."

"I think that I can guess what is coming," Fenby said, "but go on."

"Can you? He came back with my own approval stock book and showed me this block of four with the very amateur attempt to alter it. It was priced at twenty-five pounds which means that that is what I have lost by someone—Cargate, as I suspect—playing this trick on me. At least, not quite, because the other three stamps of the block remain, and together they are worth four or five pounds."

"You mean that there was a genuine no-accent variety block there before?"

"Yes. It was a sufficiently good item for me to remember it. But that isn't the end of the story. While I was looking at this, Cargate turned back to his own St. Vincents. I wasn't watching him particularly carefully, but what I now know that he did was to take out one stamp, the earliest sixpenny, which is a very distinctive deep yellow-green and is very scarce in good mint condition, and accuse me of having stolen it."

Fenby, recognizing the repetition of the trick played on Yockleton, was not in the least surprised.

"And you hadn't?" he said mildly, and without really thinking what he was saying.

"Of course I hadn't! Do you take me for a thief too?"

"No, no, no. I'm sorry. I didn't mean that. I suppose you jumped on him rather as you jumped on me."

"I did."

"And he suggested that you should be searched?"

"No, I did. How did you know that?"

"That's an interesting variation. I suppose that it was found on you?"

"It was *not!*"

"He didn't manage to palm it that time then?"

Macpherson's look of fury gradually died away.

"I see," he said. "Something of the sort occurred before

and you expected the details to be the same? I thought at first that you were contemplating believing that I had in fact removed it. Well, I don't know what the substance was that was alleged to have been stolen the first time, but a stamp is a very brittle thing and easily damaged. You can't put it loose in your pocket or drop it into your shoes—Cargate, by the way, tried the turn-ups of my trousers, but it wasn't there," Macpherson relaxed into a grin, "nor was it in my pocket-book or in any envelope in the letters in my pocket. So eventually I told him straight out that I was quite sure that he had taken it out himself and that I proposed to have no more dealings with him ever. Moreover I said that I intended to pass the word quietly round the stamp trade. At that he said that he was going to do the same about me. Well, it would have been awkward, and bringing an action against him to stop it would have only advertised it; still, I think my reputation is good enough to have stood it. But as a matter of fact I ended the controversy about that particular stamp by telling him where it was."

"Then you knew all the time? But didn't he say—?"

"Yes, he did. He said that those who hide can find, but I shouldn't have hid it in his property."

"Where was it then?" Fenby asked as Macpherson seemed to have stopped.

"In a snuffbox. At least I think it was snuff."

It most certainly was, but Fenby saw no reason to show how very much the fact interested him. Besides he rather wondered why Macpherson had pretended to be uncertain of what the contents of it was; however, he said nothing and allowed the stamp dealer to go on.

"My saying that it was in that box was a sudden inspiration and really pure guesswork on my part. You see it so happened that I had noticed this box when I came in—a heavy, valuable gold thing with a monogram on it in emeralds—rather in the same type as the Samoa issue of 1914." (Macpherson could never get away from stamps for more than five minutes at a time.) "It had been lying on the writing-table by the side of the album so that its initials were the right way up for me to read. But while we were arguing about which of us was going to blacken the other's character most effectively, I suddenly saw that the box had been inverted. So I took a shot and suggested that he looked in there—and there it was."

"Was it?" Fenby seemed to be thinking. "What happened to it then?"

"I licked a stamp mount and put it back in its place for him. I'm afraid I rather acted with intentional and obvious mock courtesy."

"You licked the mount—or the stamp?"

"The mount of course. You may lick a stamp when you put it on a letter, but if you want to keep it mint, you don't do such a thing, for fear, as they said on the margins of the Victorian penny reds, of 'damaging the cement'. I always like that phrase."

"I see. But the discovery of the stamp didn't end the argument, did it?"

"Not really. Though we pretended that it had. Because I suggested that it must have caught on his cuff when he stretched over to pick up the box and so got in accidentally. Whereupon he said 'Oh yes? I suppose I'm still lucky to have the box,' which I, in my turn, pretended not to understand. He knew very well that he had been caught out."

"Then this stamp is still there?"

"It is."

"I wonder if you would point it out to me?"

"Certainly. It's the first sixpenny in the St. Vincent collection. I should rather like to buy it if only for the fact that it is the only stamp that I have ever been accused of trying to steal."

"I'll see what I can do for you. By the way, is the back sticky?"

"I hope so. It ought to have its original gum. Of course if the gum has been replaced, it isn't so good."

"Good Lord! Do you mind about that even? And can you tell?"

"Yes. Though not always easily."

"It seems to me you must be very observant people in your line of business, so I wonder if you would tell me one other detail. Did you happen to notice if there was a bottle in the room?"

"A bottle?"

"Yes. The sort of thing you get from a chemist."

"Oh! Let me think. Yes, I rather believe that there was. Standing on the window-sill. It had a coloured label on it, red I should think, but I couldn't see properly because the label was, so to speak, on the window-pane side."

"I see. I said you were an observant man. Do you happen to remember whereabouts on the window-sill it was?"

"Let me think. The desk was in the window so that the sill served as a kind of shelf beyond it. It was to one's right as one sat at the desk. The snuffbox was on the left, on the desk itself."

"I see. Well, now, to go back to this stamp collection. I shall go and see Ley and ask him to grant your request not to do anything with it in a hurry. He can't anyhow until he has got probate and I think he will probably say that he will not act without the consent of us both, because as you rightly said, if there is a forger about, we shall be glad to help you catch him. Pretty difficult thing to prove, though. We might have to ask you to prosecute." Fenby started to go. "Oh, but just one last question. What made you say the snuffbox was heavy?"

"I don't know." Macpherson seemed rather startled by the question. "It looked it."

Fenby went away thinking of the irony of Cargate's remark that "he was lucky" still to have the box.

The movements of that snuffbox and of the bottle of potassium cyanide had interested Fenby from the first. But naturally when he had started his investigations at Scotney End Hall on the morning of July 14th he had not concentrated upon them from the outset. He had had, first of all, to make some explanation of who he was and why any investigations were necessary.

The obvious person to whom to apply had been Joan Knox Forster whom chance had left virtually in charge of the household, at any rate until Ley should arrive. Fenby conceived at once a respect for the intelligence of the tall, clumsily built, middle-aged woman who greeted him. There was a readiness about her to face facts which Fenby found extremely refreshing.

She looked at him appraisingly through powerful spectacles and quite openly summed him up.

"I don't quite understand," she said, "what you are doing. I can understand that there has to be a formal enquiry as Mr. Cargate died so suddenly, but why the Coroner should desire police investigation, I don't know. Is it usual?"

"Quite," Fenby had lied gallantly. "Merely the normal routine enquiries."

"But as to what? I mean what is there to enquire about?

The state of his health you can get best from his doctor who is in London, not down here. That he normally travelled by car, not train, I can tell you. Also that the car was really out of order on that day and that, therefore, the train journey was necessary. Again, since the gold box studded with emeralds lying on the floor of the carriage must have caught your attention, I can also assure you that he was in the habit of taking snuff just occasionally. Rather an affectation on his part, I think," she ended meditatively.

"I see. Did he have a chauffeur?" Fenby thought it best not to follow up the lead too quickly.

"No. There wouldn't be very much for him to do except wash the car and keep it in order. Hardy Hall, that's the gardener, did the washing, and apart from that he had a service contract with a garage in London to overhaul it periodically. It saved trouble. For the rest, he preferred to drive himself. I used to do a little to help in an emergency with the second car, but as it happens he had just sold the old one and the new one had not been delivered. Then again, although he liked to have someone who could act as a chauffeur when wanted, he had only just moved down here and he hadn't got things properly settled. In fact everything was in rather a muddle and there appears" (a trifle sarcastically) "to be a housing shortage in the village."

Fenby nodded.

"Let's leave out what might have been for the present and concentrate on the people who actually exist. There's this man Hall."

"No, Hardy, the only local man. Everyone down here is called Hardy—the man who gave the alarm yesterday was—and so they get nicknames. This Hardy was called Hardy Hall because he had worked at the Hall, that is here, for as long as anyone could remember. Only yesterday the vicar was trying to get Mr. Cargate to take on an under-gardener to be known as Scottish Hardy. In fact I think that that was what the row was about."

"One thing at a time, Miss Knox Forster, please. Staff first. Row with the vicar afterwards."

"Sorry. I'm not usually incoherent like this. Staff then. Myself, secretary, housekeeper and general bottle-washer. Raikes, the butler. Two housemaids. One cook, Mrs. Perriman; one kitchen-maid. I'll write down all their names for you. Outside only Hardy Hall. I've been with Mr. Cargate over a year. To be accurate since April 9th last year; Raikes, for longer. He must speak for himself. The rest are new."

"Thank you. Mr. Cargate's business?"

"Operating on the Stock Exchange. Collecting anything and everything and sometimes reselling it. There was a stamp dealer here yesterday, but stamps he collected and very seldom sold. My job was to run the house, deal with his correspondence and have ready for him facts and figures on which to base his Stock Exchange transactions."

"That's got all that clear then. Now to go back a bit. You said just now that I must have noticed the snuffbox on the floor. Actually, of course, you will remember that Dr. Gardiner had taken charge of it before I arrived. But of course he told us all about it and neither gold nor emeralds are lost." Fenby's smile deprecated the probability of the doctor stealing the box. It also helped him to bring up his next point unobtrusively. "An unusual habit that, taking snuff?"

"Yes, but it existed." Joan Knox Forster allowed herself to smile too, just in case the remark sounded like a snub.

"Where did he get his snuff from? Locally?"

"Gracious, no. He never got anything locally, a habit

which was not making him very popular down here. He got it from a firm within a stone's throw of Piccadilly Circus." She mentioned the name.

"I see. By post?"

"Yes. And since you obviously want to know, the last lot came on Wednesday, and was opened by him on Thursday morning. I happen to know because when I came into the library at a quarter to ten, the usual hour, to take down letters and receive orders, he was cursing Raikes because the inside of the snuffbox was dirty. He told him to clean it out, and when Raikes brought it back I saw him open the package and fill the box."

"So any snuff upset in the railway carriage yesterday was fresh from the makers and not opened before 9.45 a.m. on Thursday? You are quite sure of that?"

"I am. But, look here, why do you want to know?" Then before Fenby had a chance to answer she went on: "It sounds to me as if there is something behind all this and though I am a paid employee here, with no standing at all, I am more or less in charge until Mr. Ley comes. I have no desire to be obstructive in any way whatever, but I think that I ought to know a little bit more about it before you start questioning everyone like this. It's going to start them talking and it will fall on me to keep them quiet. If I were the responsible person, I shouldn't mind a bit, but as I am not, it makes it harder for me. Though I am bound to say that Mr. Ley is not the sort of man to turn on me and blame me for what I can't help. All the same—"

"I understand that very well and I really do sympathize with you, but I can promise you that you are not doing anything wrong. Perhaps I ought to take you a little more into my confidence."

"I really think that you ought. Besides," she added as Fenby seemed to be hesitating, "I'm trained to be discreet."

"Very well then. I am sure that the whole enquiry will prove to be an unnecessary precaution on our part, but Mr. Cargate did die very suddenly and so we have to make some investigation. That being so, the first thing that we see is a snuffbox and taking snuff is, as you say, an unusual habit. Moreover, the deceased was in the very act of taking a pinch of snuff when he died. There is no reason to expect that there is any connection between the two events, but we must in duty bound satisfy ourselves that there is no possibility of an accident having occurred. Besides, all this sort of facts get carefully collected together by the Home Office and sometimes it emerges from their figures that some particular substance—as it might be snuff—has unexpected dangers, and then regulations are made."

"The Home Office is very fond of grandmotherly regulations of that sort," Miss Knox Forster agreed apparently with some asperity.

"They are indeed," Fenby agreed hurriedly. He might be uttering the most unfounded slanders of the Home Office for all he knew or cared, and it was a matter of no importance whatever if he did, but it did seem to him to matter that nobody at Scotney End Hall should take his questioning as being anything other than routine, and he shrewdly considered that if he induced Joan Knox Forster to take that view, more than half his battle would be won. Beyond that he strongly disbelieved in giving anyone information that did not concern them. That ignorance was bliss was in his opinion one of the very few statements in a proverb that was ever tinged with the truth.

Accordingly he went on romancing happily and totally

belying his declared intention of taking Joan Knox Forster into his confidence.

"A great nuisance to us some of those regulations are too. But to come back to this actual case, the information you have already given us is going to be of the greatest use, because, as you can see at once, it shortens the period over which we shall have to make our enquiries. We shan't have to worry about what anyone was doing before 9.45 on Thursday morning."

"Or after Mr. Cargate left to catch the train yesterday. But, seriously, does your last remark imply that you want to know what everybody did with every minute of their time on Thursday?"

"Why, of course! I hoped that I had made that clear." Fenby opened his eyes in wide surprise and hoped, not very sanguinely, that he would get away with it. The broad grin on Miss Knox Forster's face soon undeceived him. Dr. Gardiner had been right. It was not so simple to bamboozle this apparently unimportant woman as it might have seemed.

"Don't think that I am trying to stop you for a second," she said. "So far as I'm concerned, go right ahead with it and I'll help you as much as I can, but please do not assume that I am quite mentally deficient. I do not believe for an instant that you would take all that trouble if there wasn't something that you think is wrong, something fishy which you have found out, and obviously that something is prima facie concerned with the snuff. Aren't I right?"

"How can we know anything about the snuff when the carriage that it was in was carefully washed out by the crass stupidity of the railway company yesterday?" If one was going to be untruthful, one might as well make a job of it, Fenby thought. It was all very well for Gardiner to suggest that an ally might be made of this woman, but personally

Fenby preferred no civilian allies and he would much rather have her ignorant.

Miss Knox Forster seemed not in the least surprised by his last remark. Indeed she agreed to its truth.

"But you ought not," she said, "to blame the railway company. Dr. Gardiner told them that it would be all right. I was with him at the time and perhaps I ought to have stopped him, so you can blame me equally, but it never occurred to me that it mattered."

"Pity." Fenby shook his head sadly. He hoped that the red herring had been successful and that he could now get on with his job of tracing everyone's movements with a reasonable chance of it being taken as a natural thing to do. Of course it would be simpler just to say that he intended to do so and vouchsafe no explanations at all. Very often he would have adopted that course, but on this occasion he would rather have the minimum of interest taken in what he was doing.

"It was a pity," Miss Knox Forster's voice roused him, "but if nothing is known to have been wrong with the snuff, then I am still more puzzled."

"Well, as a matter of fact"—Fenby, like many other people, used the phrase frequently to introduce a thumping lie—"it was the accident that Mr. Cargate himself bought some poison in Great Barwick which has upset the Coroner. It seems that there has been some talk of country chemists not getting their registers signed properly—"

"What a perfect mare's nest." Joan was openly laughing now. "Or rather, what a perfect wasps' nest." She went on to explain just why the potassium cyanide had been bought, while Fenby, dishonestly, allowed his face to grow longer and longer.

"It does sound," he said when she had finished, "as if I

should be wasting my time. All the same, that's all the more reason to get through it quickly."

● ● ● ● ●

"The Inspector in charge of the case, my lord, commenced by compiling a careful time-table of the activities of Mr. Cargate from the moment when the snuff was opened in the presence of Miss Knox Forster at about 9.45 until the potassium cyanide was placed in the hands of the gardener at 5.0 p.m.

"It will be part of my case that it will not be necessary to consider the period after about 3.45 p.m. when Mr. Macpherson left Mr. Cargate, but lest that fact be disputed by my learned friend, I had better recapitulate that time-table in full. It will, of course, be proved to you by various witnesses, but I think that it will simplify matters if I give it you in its entirety.

"At nine-forty-five, then, Mr. Cargate having finished his breakfast, went to his library. Miss Knox Forster came in as the clock struck, with a punctuality that was characteristic, to take down any letters which he might wish to have typed concerning his important financial transactions."

Blayton carefully glossed over the fact that they were all entirely gambling transactions of a highly speculative nature, of no value to anyone except Cargate himself, and really unnecessary even to him since he had already quite as much money as he ought to have wanted. But then, as Macpherson had implied to Fenby, if you start collecting things there is no limit to the amount which you can spend.

"The business in which Mr. Cargate was engaged was exceptionally long that morning so that Miss Knox Forster had only just finished receiving her instructions when, at a quarter to eleven, the butler announced that the Reverend Mr. Yockleton had called. Mr. Yockleton and Mr. Cargate left the library together at 11.30, but the three-quarters of an hour which then elapsed was not unimportant.

"Having seen the vicar off the premises, Mr. Cargate returned to the library where he remained by himself until about noon when, as was his custom on a fine day, he went out into the garden until luncheon at one o'clock. By about quarter to two he was back again in the library and he did not leave it again, except for the few moments during which he fetched Mr. Macpherson's stock book of stamps, until after tea—which was served to him in the library. Indeed at 5.0 p.m. he was still there, for he contented himself with beckoning to his gardener, whose name is Hardy, but who is generally known as Hardy Hall, a name which the Court may find convenient to use as distinguishing him from the witness Hardy Baker—who also derives his sobriquet from his method of earning his living—"

"Am I to understand that the name of the witness that you are going to call is Hardy or Baker?" Mr. Justice Smith had conceived an intense dislike to a sentence which was winding away interminably in parenthesis. He knew perfectly well what Blayton meant, but an imp of perverseness in him insisted that he should demand an explanation. The provision of it at any rate allowed counsel for the Crown, after giving explanations as to the peculiarities of Scotney End nomenclature, to start the sentence again.

"Beckoned, as I say, Hardy Hall, the gardener, to the window and handed out to him the bottle of poison. You will hear from this witness's own lips that it was impossible for anyone to have access to the potassium cyanide after that."

"You were instructed to take this wasps' nest?"

"I was."

"You were to use the potassium cyanide which Mr. Cargate was going to give you?"

"He was going to give me some stuff—I don't rightly know what it is called—and I was to use that."

"You knew how to use it?"

"There be a mortal lot of wopses round the Hall."

"You mean that this is not the first time that you have taken a wasps' nest?"

"Nor the twentieth. Why, in 1935, when it was so dry that there weren't no water left in the village pump and folks had to dip buckets in the moat round the Hall, I took over a dozen nests. It was a good year for wasps, that was."

"I see. I suppose you explained to Mr. Cargate that you knew all about it?"

"I did."

"And he left it all to you?"

"After a bit of talk he did. Mr. Cargate always thought he knew more than anyone else about everything."

"So he gave you directions when he gave you the bottle?"

"He'd done that before."

"Before?"

"Yes, in the morning. When Vicar had left."

"That would be about half-past eleven."

"No. It would be just before twelve."

"Are you sure?"

"Yes. It was rightly just on my dinner-time. Leastways it would be when I'd finished what I was doing. But Mr. Cargate, he didn't worry about other people's dinner-times. So I had to leave tying up the hollyhocks till after. I was right busy too and didn't want to have my time wasted being told about things I'd known since afore I was breeched."

"Quite. But he did give you some instructions?"

"He did. He puts his head out of the window and he says 'Oh, Hardy', in that rather funny sort of way he had as if speaking to you was rather an effort and hurt a bit. I likes myself to be treated as if I was a human being, but he didn't seem to see it. 'Oh, Hardy,' he says, 'I've got the stuff. I want you to fetch it to-night and then you must use it like this—' Well, I cut him short on that, because I knew. So I says—"

"Just a minute, Mr. Hardy. He pointed to the bottle?"

"That's right, on the window-sill it was. I could see the label from outside through the pane."

"You are quite sure of that?"

"Absolutely. So I said—"

"You told him you knew all about it, isn't that so? Now, it was actually at about five o'clock that he gave it to you."

"It was. I was coming up to ask him for it."

"The bottle was in the same place?"

"Yes."

"Exactly the same place? In your opinion it had not been moved at all?"

"Not so far as I knows."

"Supposing it had been moved, do you think that fact would have caught your eye?"

"Almost certain to."

"Thank you, Mr. Hardy. Then you took it away with you? And what did you do with it then?"

"I took very good care of it."

"Because it was labelled 'Poison'? Very wise of you. But just how did you do that?"

"I hid it in my tool shed till I wanted it in the evening. Tool shed's locked every night in case of tramps and I will say for Mr. Cargate that he'd let me have a new key. Besides that, I put it away right at the back, same as I always do lest someone should come round interfering. No one would find it easily unless they knew where to look."

"You took all these precautions in case some unauthorized person got hold of the poison?"

"That be right. I was always taught to be careful of nasty things like that."

"This was just after five o'clock?"

"It was. I locked up and went off to my tea. Then in the evening I came back and fetched it, and went and took wasps' nest. Then I put it back again safe."

"You didn't use it all?"

"No. Mr. Cargate knew mighty little about wasps' nests whatever he may have said and he'd bought a sight too much of it. So I put it back and locked it up again, and a mottal nuisance it was because I couldn't get Mr. Cargate the next morning to take it back. I did try to speak to him, but he was busy, what with going up to London and so forth, so I had to keep the tool shed locked till I could get him. And of course I never did that because he was killed that day. So I kept it until the police chap came and right glad I was to give it to him."

"You had to keep the tool shed locked until you got rid of the poison?"

"That's what I've been telling you."

"I just wanted to make it quite clear. Now, you never gave any of the poison to anyone during that time?" A violent shake of the head, coupled with an amazed look, was the only answer. "No one asked you for any?"

"Of course not. Why, whatever are you a-thinking of?"

"And the bottle was never disturbed?"

"It were always where I put it."

"Thank you, Mr. Hardy."

Mr. Vernon got up to cross-examine on behalf of the defence.

"Which way did you put the bottle down when it was in the shed?"

"Behind a sight of other things. Small tools and twine, and stuff for spraying things and such-like."

"I see. With the label facing towards you so that you could see it and be warned by it?"

"Label was clear anyhow."

"It showed up pretty distinctly in whatever position the bottle was? So that in the shed it did not matter whether it faced anyone looking for it or not?" A series of nods. "But are you certain whether it was facing you or not?"

Hardy scratched his head.

"I'm not rightly certain. I think it were."

"Yet, although you are not certain as to its exact position when it was in your care, you are positive as to exactly how it stood when you saw it through glass and it did not really matter to you how it stood?"

"It were dark in the shed."

"And light on the window-sill; so that the bright label would show up more clearly, even if it was actually not facing you but facing away from you into the library?"

"It were facing me."

"When you saw it the first time, at twelve o'clock, you were in a hurry to get away to your dinner?"

"I was."

"And are you quite sure that when you saw it the second time at five o'clock, it was in exactly the same place?"

"I believe it were."

"You believe it. I'm sure you do, but are you absolutely

certain? Might it not have been moved quite a small fraction without your noticing? Supposing that somebody had picked it up and put it down again as far as possible in the same place, would you have known that?"

"Perhaps not."

"Exactly, Mr. Hardy. Now, to turn to your tool shed. Do you usually keep it locked? I don't mean all night; I mean during the day-time when you are working there?"

"Not when I'm working. I locks it when I goes away."

"Very prudent. But the next morning, after you had taken this wasps' nest; are you sure that you locked it then?"

"I was very careful that morning, 'cos you see the stuff was inside."

"I see. Thank you, Mr. Hardy." Vernon thought that he had better be satisfied with the little that he had got.

"Just a minute, Mr. Hardy." Blayton was on his feet again. "You told us that on both occasions the bottle was facing you. Can you give any reason why you are certain of that?"

A moment's pause ensued while Blayton wondered if he could extract the information that he wanted without asking a question so leading that it might cause his lordship to intervene. Slowly, however, an idea seemed to be coming to Hardy.

"It must have been facing me. How else could I have read the word 'Poison'?"

"That is all, thank you." Blayton, with a sigh of relief, sat down.

"Not quite, I am afraid." Vernon was up again. "That is, my lord, if you will allow me to put a few further questions arising out of what has just been elicited by my learned friend? You have seen," he went on as Mr. Justice Smith nodded assent, "a label of that colour before with the word 'poison' on it?"

"I've taken many wopses' nests that way."

"And you were expecting to be given this poison?"

"Mr. Cargate had told me he would get it."

"Thank you. I believe that that really is all now."

Wisely or unwisely Fenby had never seriously considered the doubts which Vernon was later on to develop as to the possibility of Hardy Hall being right at least as to his statement that from five o'clock onwards the potassium cyanide had been available for himself only.

The possibility that the gardener was himself concerned could not of course be entirely dismissed as absolutely out of the question; still, it was so improbable that virtually it could be ignored. For one thing a very few enquiries showed that while he might have got at the poison, he could not have obtained access to the snuff. There was undoubtedly the possibility of collusion with, for example, Raikes, but, for the time being, Fenby thought that he might safely confine himself to the period between 9.45 a.m. and 5.0 p.m.

During that time he would want to find out all that he could about the movements of all the people concerned and also of two things, namely the bottle of potassium cyanide and the snuffbox itself. It would, he felt, be best to begin with the people since in the course of that the things might fit themselves into place, and perhaps the easiest person on whom to start was Miss Knox Forster herself. She would for one thing be certain to answer clearly; for another she would provide a yard-stick with which to clarify what other people had been doing—incidentally Cargate's own movements would be discovered from what she said—and finally, if she consented, no one else could very well refuse.

It proved at least to be an idea that was quite simple to carry out in one respect—Miss Knox Forster herself not only was quite prepared to do it, she had apparently been expecting it.

"In fact ever since you turned up, I have been marshalling my thoughts so as to give you an orderly description. From 9.45 until the vicar was shown in I was taking down letters and so forth—that was the normal routine. It usually went on longer but Mr. Yockleton came at about a quarter to eleven and stayed until nearly half-past. I spent about half an hour of that in typing some of the letters which had been dictated to me and then, so as to be handy when I was wanted, because the vicar had interrupted us before Mr. Cargate had finished, I got some flowers from the garden and started to do the roses in the hall. It's not a job that I always do—to tell you the truth I do it rather badly—but there were dead things on the oak table in the middle, and I was afraid that if Mr. Cargate saw them there might be an explosion. Explosions were pretty frequent in that direction.

"Therefore I saw Mr. Yockleton leave. Mr. Cargate walked out with him and as to what was happening, perhaps you will ask him. Anything I know is only a rumour, but I think that there had been another explosion starting with the parish and ending with the snuffbox."

"Oh, where was that then?"

"Raikes had brought it back while I was dictating letters and it was on the side table, I think. No, on the desk by Mr. Cargate's right hand. That is when I left. I think Mr. Cargate picked it up himself later and I forget where he put it down. The same place, I think, but I don't remember properly."

"This bottle with the potassium cyanide must have looked odd beside it." Fenby tried to sound casual.

"Oh, you want to know about that too, do you? It was on the window-sill all day I believe. At least I saw it there when I went out to get some roses. You could see it from the garden."

Fenby nodded.

"I think you said that Mr. Cargate walked away with Mr. Yockleton, didn't you? Did he come back again?"

"Oh, yes, in quite a few minutes. Between five and ten I should say. Then he came back again and stayed in the library until midday."

"Just a minute. During those few minutes anyone could have gone into the library?"

Miss Knox Forster thought a minute.

"In a way, yes. But either I or Raikes, who was going backwards and forwards to the dining-room, were about most of the time, and anyone quite strange I think we must have noticed. One of the maids would not have excited comment but I don't remember seeing one."

"How long an interval do you think that there was when neither of you were there?"

"Let me see. I was in the hall when Mr. Cargate went out. Then I went to get one more rose from that bed there." She pointed to where on the lawn in front of the windows of the library some low bushes of deep crimson roses were growing sturdily in the heavy clay soil. "It took a little searching to find just what I wanted as I had picked some from there already and I didn't want to spoil the appearance of the bed. Perhaps it took a minute and a half. Raikes had been in the dining-room when I went out. Just as I came back he went out through the door." She pointed to the back of the hall and added that as he must have passed through the hall it lessened the time when anyone could go unobserved into the library.

"After that," she went on, "I finished doing that bowl

there—the crimson shows up well against the panelling, doesn't it?—and went to see if the ones in the drawing-room were all right. None of them had died, so I came back just as Mr. Cargate returned."

"I see." Fenby looked round the big hall. The door of the dining-room was on the right as you came in at the front door facing that leading into the library. On the same side as the library, a little farther on, was the door to the drawing-room, opposite which the hall widened out to the right and gave access both to the stairs with their old oak balustrade, and to a small room beyond the dining-room which Miss Knox Forster explained was her sitting-room and in which she worked. The table on which stood the bowl of roses had been placed in the centre of the broader part of the hall, and by it Fenby went and stood.

It was a fairly long oak, gate-legged table so that while anyone standing at the end nearest to the drawing-room could see the doors of both the library and the dining-room, anyone at the far end was prevented by the angle of the wall from seeing more than part of the library door. All the same a figure coming out of the library would probably be visible—that is, unless whoever stood there was too intent on arranging the roses. As for the door leading to the kitchen, it faced the front door and could be seen from any point in the hall.

"I don't believe," Fenby said, "that anyone could go into the library without your noticing it."

"Not while I was here."

"Now, could anyone go in without being observed by Raikes in the dining-room?"

"I should think, yes, but let's look."

Fenby walked into the dining-room and at once saw that

Miss Knox Forster was right. The door was opposite to that of the library, it was true, but it was at the side of the room so that while Raikes had been moving round the table he would have seen the part of the hall outside the drawing-room, but he could not have looked into the library unless he had moved from the table to the door.

A buzzing attracted Fenby to the window on which a quantity of wasps showed that not all the wasps' nests round Scotney End Hall had been taken.

"But what can you expect," Miss Knox Forster read his thoughts. "The garden wall running out from my room faces due south, as you see, and the apricots and peaches are just beginning to think about getting ripe. Consequently, despite our muslin and such-like precautions, every wasp in the county comes to eat them, green though they are, and then drops in for a little marmalade for a change. They're a perfect curse, but you can't have everything."

"No." All the same Fenby seemed to like looking out at the garden, at the great formal bed of yellow and white roses in front of the dining-room window and the corresponding bed of crimson ones on the other side that were not so easy to see unless you looked right out. "Very well then," he said, coming apparently suddenly out of a reverie. "For that short period we can dismiss anyone but you and Raikes; very largely you clear Raikes except for the minute and a half when you picked the rose, and the short period when you went to the drawing-room."

"A minute and a half, once more, I suppose. And in the first case I might have been able to see in through the window; but as you see Raikes can't clear me."

"Not entirely."

"Except that he might have heard." Suddenly Joan Knox

Forster laughed. "Mr. Fenby, do you really want me to believe that these are just routine investigations? Is as much trouble as this always taken?"

"Well, perhaps not. All the same I expect it will prove to be nothing more than that in the end. Still, I think that we have spent quite long enough considering those few minutes. When Mr. Cargate returned, you saw him?"

"Yes; he said that I was to finish my typing, and I got on with it until midday when he rang for me. It was his custom to be out from twelve to one if the day was at all decent, but he had not finished his letters. So he decided to do both things at once by sitting under the elm trees there and dictating to me. He was in rather a bad temper, partly because he didn't agree with what Mr. Yockleton had been saying and partly because he had been trying to explain to Hardy Hall how to take a wasps' nest and Hardy had cut him short. Mr. Cargate always thought that he knew more about anything than anybody else. He was, to be honest, a frightful bore when he was in one of his lordly moods, so I got him out of the house as quickly as I could and settled him under the trees and there we stayed till lunch time."

"So anybody could have gone into the library during that hour so far as you know."

"Anybody from inside but not, I think, from outside. I couldn't actually see the front door but I could see part of the garden in front of the house and most of the path leading up to it."

"You went back to the house for lunch at one?"

"Yes. Mr. Cargate said that he was hungry and we both went straight in. I was rather cross with him because he didn't wash. I do insist on cleanliness personally, even if I don't care much about personal appearances."

"You had lunch with him?"

"Yes."

"During that time the door was shut and you couldn't see into the library?"

"Quite."

"So that from twelve noon until—when?—you can't really help me?"

"We finished lunch about 1.45. No, during that period, I can't. Except as to my own movements."

"And after that?"

"Mr. Cargate went back to the library and I don't think that he went out of it again, except to get the stamp collection, until after tea. He gave the bottle which you seem to be interested in to Hardy Hall round about five o'clock."

"How do you know that?"

"Because Hardy came to the window of my room and asked me to help him. He wanted to get the bottle and go and Mr. Cargate wouldn't take any notice of him, so he thought that I might pull his chestnuts out of the fire for him, but I'm afraid that I refused. The day had been quite stormy enough as it was. So Hardy stamped up and down the lawn until Mr. Cargate did condescend to notice him. He didn't do it very quickly because I think that he was still angry with him for cutting him short earlier in the day. In fact I think that he ended by saying that if Hardy got stung by a large number of infuriated wasps, it would serve him right for not listening to good advice when it was given to him."

For the moment Fenby decided, on an intuition which subsequently proved to be right, not to worry about what happened later on that day. Instead he changed the subject completely.

"I understand that you told Dr. Gardiner that you know something about his will?"

"Yes. By the way, from the point of view of the nation, it's a good thing that he died."

"Well," Fenby assented cautiously, "Mr. Ley did tell me something about it. But I gather that that was not the motive which prompted Mr. Cargate."

"It certainly was not. You should have heard him on economics! He used to produce some quite remarkable paradoxes, with which I, as an intellectual woman of the left-centre with a definite anti-war bias, strongly disagreed. He used, for instance, to say that the tax which bore most hardly on the poor was the sur-tax."

"But why? They don't pay it."

"No, but making the rich pay it throws the poor out of work or prevents them getting decent wages, so he said. The objection to the theory seems to be that I have never heard that wages were higher before the introduction of the sur-tax. Another thing Mr. Cargate always held was that until you made the rich not only rich but oppressively and disgustingly rich, you had no hope of producing anything other than poverty for the poor. I asked him why once and his reply was: 'Because we are all parasites in one way or another. I, in a big way; you, in a smaller way.' I am bound to say that it was not one of his more tactful remarks."

"It doesn't sound it."

"I suppose it was because he was so innately selfish and entirely self-centred that he was almost invariably tactless, because I don't think that he meant to be. However, to go back to his economic ideas; he used to say that the one thing that did no good to the nation was spending by the Government and that direct taxation was the root of all evil. There was some simile about taking the water away from the source of the river instead of letting it first turn the mills farther downstream, but I think that that is not only far-fetched, but false. Anyhow, it's eighty years old because I found it in Allison's *History of Europe*."

Never having read that long and ponderous work Fenby did not attempt to argue.

"I can understand," he said, "your not agreeing with him if you are left-centre minded, so to speak, but what's an anti-war bias got to do with it?"

"Well, he supported rearmament."

"I shouldn't have thought that he would from what you tell me, since it involves Government expenditure. And, even so, rearmament has got nothing to do with war."

"Oh, hasn't it? Let me tell you that nothing would permit me ever to go to war again. It's nothing but licensed murder."

"A great many people feel like that now, I know, and other people feel that by so thinking they will produce the exact opposite result to what they desire. There's a great deal to be said on both sides—or at any rate a great deal is said—but to go back, why should he approve of rearmament?"

"He said that it was completely useless and therefore very valuable." Joan Knox Forster shook her head. "Beyond me. I suppose he wasn't mad, was he?"

"It's the first time that I have heard the suggestion and as I never met him, I am hardly the person to ask."

"No. I just wondered."

● ● ● ● ●

"A nasty business, Raikes, and one which I dare say you do not like talking over."

"Very nasty, sir. No doubt you have been told that I couldn't bring myself to touch the—the door on which he was."

"I had heard something about it. You had been in his service for some time, hadn't you?"

"Yes, and despite his little tricks and a lot of funny ways that he had, I had a considerable respect for him. He had a way of saying, so to speak: 'Take it or leave it,' so that you knew where you were with him which made it easy to handle him if you knew how."

"And you did know how to handle him?"

"I venture to think so, sir." There was a quiet confidence about the elderly butler which was totally removed from conceit. "I suppose," he went on unexpectedly, "that it was his heart that made him funny."

"Funny?" Fenby echoed.

"Well, sir, if you knew that you might die at any moment, you'd look at things differently. When you saw other people fussing and getting into a state about things that upset them, and all the time you knew that you had got one thing real to worry about, you'd rather despise them and not worry much if you trod on their corns. In fact you would rather like to give them something to think about. At any rate that's what I think that he did, and then people would say that he was tactless, and hard, and inconsiderate, and ought to do this and ought not to have done the other. The village people round here, for instance. They're stupid and they didn't understand him, and that vicar, he would keep on interfering and making things worse. Miss Knox Forster, she didn't understand him either and she's got very strong views, and just to annoy her he used to take the opposite view and then they'd start arguing about politics and things and she never knew that he was pulling her leg."

"Then you don't think that he always meant what he said?"

"Not he. If you come to think of it, it was a plucky thing

the way that he kept up all his hobbies—making money and collecting stamps like a kid and so on. All the same his tricks were trying if you didn't know how to meet them. That is when he was in the mood."

"What sort of tricks? Do you mean just the way he went on in general or have you got something particular in your mind?"

"One particular little game that he was always playing. He used to have days when he liked to pretend that people were trying to steal things from him. When that mood was on him, he would do it all day to everyone who came near him, and a great nuisance it was too. I suppose he went a bit funny sometimes. Personally I always knew when it was coming on and so I took precautions, but those who didn't know it, used to find it troublesome, because he was clever about it. It wasn't exactly conjuring but he would put things where you didn't expect them to be, and it wasn't easy to prove that he had done it. And last Thursday, the day you want to know about, was one of those days. I saw it coming on."

"Oh!" This was a new development to Fenby. "What were the signs?"

"He sent for me first thing after breakfast and told me to clean the snuffbox. Now it was a gold one and it didn't really want cleaning and so I looked at it a bit surprised, which he noticed. So he says something about the inside which, if you will pardon my saying so, was pure poppycock. However, I took it away and pretended, and then I saw that the big emerald on the lid was loose and I says to myself 'Alfred, my lad, somebody is going to be accused of stealing that, but it isn't going to be you. Or, if it is, you are going to be able to prove that it wasn't.' So when I brought it back, I put it down on the table by his left hand where both he and

Miss Knox Forster could see it clearly. In fact I pushed that emerald under both their noses, and furthermore I made up my mind that I was going to be able to prove that from that time on I hadn't been in that room by myself for the whole of the rest of the day."

"By his left hand?" Fenby looked at his notes.

"Yes. Let me show you." Raikes started to lead the way from the dining-room across to the library and then politely asked Fenby to go first. "Just here."

"I see." Fenby made a note. "Go on."

"The next time that I came in was to show the vicar in. Miss Knox Forster left when he arrived. Then I went on with my duties. First of all cleaning the silver and then laying the table for lunch."

"You were still doing that when the vicar left?"

"I was in the dining-room then and he called me out and spoke to me sharp-like about the clock. All nonsense it was but that was a bit awkward because the library door was left open when they went out and I didn't see how I could prove that I hadn't been in and I could see from Mr. Cargate's face that I was right. He *was* in one of his moods. However, luck was with me because Miss Knox Forster was in the hall. I talked to her too for a bit about the clock. I should have liked to have gone on but she didn't seem to want to. She was just putting those roses right. Beautiful sweet-scented ones, aren't they, sir? Étoile d'Hollande, they call them."

"Yes, but go on." Fenby refused to be side-tracked into horticultural details. Moreover Raikes's pronunciation of the name was such as to convey at most, nothing to him. "Miss Knox Forster was in the hall?"

"Yes, sir. So I had only to stay in the dining-room and she would be able to say that I had not gone out. At least so I thought, but as a matter of fact when I did leave, just as Mr. Cargate came back, she was in the drawing-room, so perhaps it wouldn't have been so good an alibi as I thought. Of course it didn't matter as he never did try to say that I had tried to take the emerald at that time. Only, of course, I didn't know that then, so that though it isn't of any importance, it did worry me at the time. Especially in view of what happened later."

"Just a minute. Let me see. I forget if Miss Knox Forster says that she went out once before that or not. Did you hear her?"

"No, sir. At least she didn't pass the door of the dining-room while I was in it. I should not have seen her but I think that I must have heard her."

Fenby thought a minute. It was possible of course that her movements had been so quiet as not to attract attention, but he would like to try an experiment or two before he was certain that it was probable. Before, however, he said anything, Raikes went on:

"Of course putting down spoons and forks does make a little noise, though I do not bang these about and scratch like some young people do nowadays."

"Are you quite sure that Miss Knox Forster was in the drawing-room when you left? She seems to think that you had gone some few minutes earlier."

"Quite certain. Actually I heard Mrs. Perriman, that is the cook, sir, come to the door leading from the kitchen to the hall a few minutes before and call softly to me—I rather wonder at her doing that with Miss Knox Forster about but I suppose she was at the end of the table near the staircase, and Cook didn't see her because of the door itself. I didn't answer until I saw that Mr. Cargate was just on back and then I went out and I distinctly saw Miss Knox Forster in the drawing-room. Some dead flowers had left a stain at the bottom of a glass bowl, I suppose, because she was trying to clean out the bottom of it. I can show you the scratch there is on it."

"We'll look at it later, but go on now." Fenby had no doubt that when Raikes left finally Miss Knox Forster had been in the drawing-room. Also it was possible that she had assumed that the door closing behind Mrs. Perriman had been closing behind Raikes and that, immersed in looking at the bowl in the drawing-room, she had not heard Raikes go. If that was so, it rather strengthened the possibility of her admitted movement to fetch the rose having been inaudible to Raikes. Still, it was a matter to be considered further and it would be interesting to see what Mrs. Perriman would say. He tried a few more questions to Raikes but without any further information.

"So at some time between 11.35 and 11.40 you went back to the kitchen?"

"That's right, sir. Now, sir, I got a bit of a shock when I found that Miss Knox Forster hadn't been in the hall all the time, because you see I wanted to be able to prove to Mr. Cargate that I hadn't been near the snuffbox. So when I went back I says to Mrs. Perriman that he's in one of his moods. 'Now,' I says, 'he's as regular as clockwork. He won't stir out of that library until twelve o'clock and that's the time that we have our dinner. So I want you to take very careful note that I don't go out of here from now on until we've finished our dinner.' 'Why, whatever for?' says Mrs. Perriman. So then I explains to her carefully and she says 'Very well, Mr. Raikes, I will, and when you go to ring the gong for lunch' (we had a gong so that Mr. Cargate could hear if he was in the garden) 'I'll go with you and watch you, so that I can say that you haven't been in that library.' You can always trust Mrs. Perriman to play up properly and help you. A real good sort she is."

Fenby, sincerely hoping that Mrs. Perriman's loyalty confined itself to the limits of the truth, assented politely to the flattering description of the cook.

"So she watched you ring the gong?"

"Yes. Mr. Cargate and Miss Knox Forster were on the lawn at the side of the house and they came round to the front door. Lunch was cold that day and Mr. Cargate preferred, if possible, to have everything on the table and not to be waited on, so I didn't have to be there until he rang to bring the sweet in."

"I should have thought that he was the sort of man who would have wanted you dancing attendance on him all the time."

"Some days he would and some days he wouldn't. This was a day when it was 'wouldn't', I could see. So I stayed away. Well, anyhow, I gave them a few minutes to wash and settle down and then I said to Mrs. Perriman—"

"Just a minute. They were pretty quick, weren't they?"

"Oh, just the ordinary time. Where was I? Oh, yes, I said to Mrs. Perriman: 'Now, you can't be watching me all the time that they are having lunch, there being a hot chocolate *soufflé* to follow, so directly they're in, you come along with me and we'll turn the key in the library door and you can keep it until they're due to come out. Just before that, we'll unlock it together. Then I can't have been in there and he can't accuse you and anyhow, Dolly' (that's the kitchen-maid, sir), 'will have been with you, so that will be all right. And after we've opened it again, we'll keep in each other's sight until he's gone back to the library.' So we did that."

"I see. Rather elaborate precautions, weren't they?"

"You didn't know Mr. Cargate. They proved to have been necessary."

"They did, did they?"

"They did. I didn't have to worry much for the rest of the afternoon because Mr. Cargate himself was in the library all afternoon. I did go in to show in a man called Macpherson, I think, a stamp dealer. He was fetched up after lunch from Larkingfield by Miss Knox Forster and it was while she was putting the car away in the garage, by the way, sir, that the first signs of something going wrong with it appeared—and so I had no occasion to go to the library until I took in the tea."

"Just a minute." Fenby scribbled down a note to remind himself that he had not asked Miss Knox Forster what she had done with herself all the afternoon. It was probably of no importance as Cargate himself had been in the library all afternoon, he understood. As yet he had not heard of the short interval during which Macpherson had been left alone by himself. "You took in the tea. Yes, and what happened then?"

"There was, sir, rather a painful scene."

"Oh, there was, was there? Your expectations were justified then?"

"Yes, sir. But not in the exact manner that I expected. Mr. Cargate started by telling me that it was an extraordinary thing but that everybody was trying to steal his property that day in some way or another. That of course was the line which I had expected that he would take. When he went on to say that Mr. Yockleton had tried to filch the emerald, I was not surprised. That was just the way that things did take him, nor did it astonish me when he began to describe what he termed a plot by this Macpherson to ruin his stamp collection, but then he went on to say that Miss Knox Forster and I were jointly in league with him. That, sir, would have been impossible. Miss Knox Forster, though she happens to be a lady, or very nearly one, and at any rate has always been treated as such, really only ranks as a governess or as a typist in an office, and is not the sort of person with whom I would associate. Besides, so far as Mr. Cargate's household was concerned, she was a comparative new-comer who did not really understand him at all."

The view was not one with which Fenby entirely concurred, but he saw no reason to argue about it.

"Then I may take it, that there was nothing in Mr. Cargate's suggestion of this league against him?"

"Naturally not, sir."

"Did he offer any evidence in support of his idea?"

"I regret to say that he did, sir." During the pause while Raikes was collecting his thoughts, Fenby had time to wonder exactly where the butler placed him in the social scale. Did he too rank as a governess, as something really inferior to the upper servants? Very likely he did and he must not set too much store by the occasional 'sir' and the outward deference paid to him, for as much or more had been given to Miss Knox Forster without there being any real respect.

"You *regret* to say?" he prompted, abandoning the point as immaterial, but finding that Raikes was slow to go on.

"Yes, sir. It led up to that point of the interview which proved to be painful. Mr. Cargate first of all stated that everything in his room kept on being moved about. The place in the book which he had been reading had been lost; the letter which he had in his hand when Mr. Yockleton had arrived and which he had put down by the side of the bottle containing the poison for the wasps' nest, when he returned from seeing the vicar, was somewhere else, and the bottle which had been on the table was on the window-sill with the word 'Poison' staring at him. He said that it annoyed him and he turned it round. Then he accused Macpherson of tampering with his stamp album and of turning the snuffbox the other way round, so that the initials were upside down. He said, and that was certainly true, that untidiness of that sort irritated him. He never could bear seeing anything the wrong way up. How much truth there was in all that, I do not know. Probably none, because there was nothing in what he said next."

"Which was?"

"That I had been in the room between midday when he went out into the garden and the end of lunch. He said that there was a stink—I am sorry, sir, but that was the word he used, and that the snuffbox had again been moved."

"Did he say what kind of stink?"

"No, sir. Nor did I ask. Nor again did I enquire in what way I was supposed to have moved the box. I am afraid, sir, that I immediately denied the insinuation, and I went on to tell him that I could prove that I had not been in the room. On that he, of course, asked how I could do that and I told him, though more briefly, exactly what I have told you as to my movements. It was, you see, exactly what I had been expecting in a sense and so I had it all ready for him and incidentally for you. But, unfortunately, it had a very deplorable effect on Mr. Cargate, very deplorable indeed. He seemed to think that it reflected on his character, as in a way I suppose it did" (the truth of the idea seemed only just to have occurred to Raikes) "and he resented it very strongly. He said that I was a smug, suspicious, self-righteous Paul Pry and other things which I would not like to repeat, and that he would have no one in his service who held the views about him that my actions seem to suggest, that he hadn't an honest or a decent friend in the world, and then he got into a state of mind in which in all my long experience of him I have never seen him get before. He began to cry."

"Self-pity, I suppose," Fenby suggested.

"I imagine so, and very painful it was, very. To see a gentleman for whom with all his faults I had always had a considerable respect behaving like that was not a thing that I cared for at all. Of course he ended by saying that he could not bear to have me about any more and finally gave me the sack. That was better—it was behaving more like a man, or at least it would have been if he had done it in anger. But he didn't, he did it in sorrow, saying that he had had one honest man about him and now he had got to lose him. Considering how free he had been with his accusations in the past and what he had obviously just been going to say, it was pretty silly, but I tried to forgive him. In fact all that evening I tried to bring myself to overlook it and carry on."

"But it was *he* was giving *you* the sack."

"That didn't mean a thing. He had done that half a dozen times before and neither of us took any notice of it. The question was whether I should give him notice. I was just trying to make up my mind when he left to go up to London, and I'd very nearly decided," Raikes's voice broke, "that I never could imagine things being the same as they had been before, when the news came through that he was dead. Then I felt that I had been in a way disloyal to him and that it was too late to do anything about it. That really was the reason I couldn't bring myself to help to carry him into the house."

"I see."

There were many little details that Fenby wanted to fill in

but for the moment he decided that he would prefer first to digest what he had obtained and to compare Raikes's statements with what he had been told by Miss Knox Forster. Also there was Mrs. Perriman to interview, and the gardener, and the vicar. For the moment therefore he finished with Raikes.

It was a constant complaint of Inspector Fenby's that he had to spend a great part of his time examining some subject which proved in the end to be irrelevant. He was always on the look-out for the danger and he tried hard to avoid entangling himself in such things. But you could never be sure. There were frequent traps. Certainly the actions of those concerned during the long central period of Thursday, July 12th were a good example of such a state of affairs.

On the whole Mr. Blayton summed the matter up accurately.

"We now come, my lord and members of the jury, to the long period in the day to which I have previously referred. You will remember that I said that it lasted from 12.0 noon until 1.45 p.m., but that there was an important exception to that period. That exception is, broadly speaking, that for nearly all of that hour and three quarters, the library almost certainly was not entered by anyone. Indeed from noon until the gong was rung for lunch by Raikes, it is improbable that anyone could have entered from outside without being seen by Mr. Cargate himself as well as Miss Knox Forster, and Mr. Cargate was, as you will hear, in a very suspicious state that day.

"During that time, that is roughly from noon until one, the indoor servants were together in the servants' hall partaking of their dinner. You will have the unimpeachable testimony of Mrs. Perriman, the cook, and of Dolly Jones the kitchen-maid, that they were all together for that period.

It may then nearly, but not quite, be dismissed from your minds. Further, from one until one-forty-five peculiar precautions were taken at the instigation of Raikes, which resulted in the library door being locked from the time that Mr. Cargate sat down to lunch until just before he finished, and during that time there is no doubt but that the key was in Mrs. Perriman's pocket, nor is there any evidence to show that any attempt to enter by the window was made. Indeed such a thing would have been difficult to carry out without leaving traces on the window, or the window-sill, or on the flower-bed, not that which contained the crimson roses, but a narrower bed immediately adjoining the side of the house, and though very careful investigations were made, no such traces were found.

"At first glance, therefore, you might think that this whole period might be dismissed from our reckoning owing to the doubts which Raikes conceived and the precautions which he took as a result of those fears. But, members of the jury, when you have heard the whole story, you will be too astute to assume so much without further consideration, and you will be right. For there were at least two periods during that time, each of only a few moments, when the library might have been entered. The first begins at the moment when Mr. Cargate and Miss Knox Forster left the garden, and lasts, not only until they are seated in the dining-room, but even really until Mrs. Perriman has turned the key in the door of the library. Similarly there is a gap after the door is unlocked until in fact Mr. Cargate leaves the dining-room, for Mrs. Perriman must be back in her own part of the house before Mr. Cargate finishes his coffee and she has to make an estimate of when that will be.

"It will be part of my case that one of those periods was

of material importance, namely, the few minutes that elapsed while Mr. Cargate…"

But it was a long while before Fenby had reached that point. At first he had not shown the astuteness which Blayton attributed to the jury so glibly and probably so unwisely since it irritated the foreman at least. At first he had considered that when Mrs. Perriman and Dolly Jones fully bore out all Raikes's statement, that the whole hour and three quarters might be dismissed from the scope of his investigations and he had gone on to see Hardy Hall, the gardener.

There had been a slight break there because Ley had at length arrived. Fenby had been in the garden when his car drew up at the front door and he had wondered whether the solicitor would remember that they were not supposed to have met before. His doubts were however immediately dispelled by hearing Ley ask who he was and then, seeing him, bustle across to him.

"So you are looking into things for the Coroner, are you? Excellent, excellent. Nothing to enquire into of course, but always a good thing to do." Like all amateurs Ley began to overact sadly. In addition it seemed to occur to him that had Fenby been in doubt in reality as to whether there was anything which needed investigation, perhaps the remark would not have been completely soothing to his feelings. At any rate he fussily covered it over with an offer to provide any assistance that lay within his power and, still apparently finding the going treacherous, turned aside with assumed heartiness to compliment Hardy Hall upon his roses.

"Very fine they are. Very fine indeed. Of course this heavy soil of yours—Still, I must try to grow some of those myself. I like that semi-double loose petal variety. What are they? K. of K.? Yes, yes, I'll make a note of it. A very fine second bloom.

Not much smell though." He fussed off having broken the train of Fenby's thought completely.

Hardy Hall too had viewed him with contempt.

"Roses wouldn't grow for such as him," was his comment. "You want patient people who understand. Second bloom indeed! This is July and you don't get the second bloom till September! Why, not one of these has been picked this year."

Fenby raised his eyebrows slightly and returned to the question of wasps' nests, a subject which, as Hardy was a man of few words, was soon exhausted. It was not very long before he was down at the rectory contemplating the vicar's bald head and broad blue eyes. There was something very likeable about the Reverend Mr. Yockleton, he decided, or at least there would be if he was not so anxious to show it. Perhaps too it would have been better if he had not been so patently desirous of being regarded as a broad-minded man, capable of much more than just looking after mothers' meetings, but rather as one really able to rule and direct men and the affairs of much bigger places than the village of Scotney End. Fenby could easily see what Raikes had meant when he referred to him as "interfering". Yes, it might be of interest to study the vicar's character, and it had better be done by discussing the matter in hand. He threw out a question and began to receive more information as to the vicar's state of mind than as to the events that had occurred, for Yockleton was still worried and anxious to justify his conscience as to the indecent joy that he still felt, that Cargate was no longer the Squire of Scotney End.

It was, therefore, a very detailed account that Fenby received of the local feeling and prejudice—he had to hear for instance all about Scottish Hardy's adventures, which to Fenby's mind were beside the point, and about the checks to the vicar's authority. Once more Fenby found himself up against the old difficulty of separating what was material from what was not, and patiently he absorbed it all in case there should be some detail which would illuminate the whole. Then he turned the current of the vicar's narrative on to the subject of what had passed between him and Cargate two days before. Yockleton, he found, was still angry, and if possible even more anxious to inveigh against Cargate's preposterous allegation that he had contemplated stealing the emerald.

"Though really why I should worry to defend myself, I don't know," he ended, changing his tone to some extent. "Everyone knows that I am the last person who is likely to do such a thing."

Fenby agreed politely, although he could not help thinking that "everyone" did not in fact include himself. He knew really very little about Yockleton and he was not quite sure how he was going to find out more. Probably the best plan would be to go into the village inn and try to discover what the parishioners of Scotney End thought.

But for the moment that must wait, and he turned back again to the question of the position of the snuffbox and the bottle. On these points Yockleton was quite definite. The snuffbox had been on the left-hand side of the table and the bottle had been quite close to it. In each case, so Yockleton averred, Cargate himself had mentioned their position. Fenby listened with interest to the categorical statements. The trouble about them was that they were so very cut-and-dried. It was Fenby's experience that it was not always those who were most unequivocal in their assertions who were always the most accurate.

By the time that he left the vicarage, he was really only sure of two things; in the first place that undoubtedly there had been a time when Yockleton had been alone with the poison and the snuff, and secondly that it was now Saturday evening, and that it was unlikely he would be able to get back to London that night. On the whole his best plan seemed to be to return on Sunday and pay a call on the stamp dealer, Macpherson, on the Monday. After that it would depend on circumstances, but probably he would have to return again to Scotney End. So far he did not feel that he had any clear idea of what had happened and yet he felt that when he had digested everything that he had been told, that somewhere in the mass of information he had obtained, were the few facts that really mattered.

Meanwhile the village inn was inviting from the point of view of pleasure and of duty. Nor did it prove difficult to find out what Scotney End thought of Yockleton. They liked him though some of them did entertain the opinion that it was unnecessary for him to try to arrange all their lives for them. Raikes they considered to be unnecessarily stand-offish. As to Miss Knox Forster they had not made up their mind, but none of them, though they did not say so in so many words, were sorry that Cargate was no longer at the Hall.

Finally, refreshed both in body and mind, Fenby went back to see Ley. The solicitor, he found, had also decided to stay the night at Scotney End. He had not had much difficulty in inventing an excuse to Miss Knox Forster to justify his lingering there—there were plenty of papers to be looked through—but it was fairly clear that he really hoped to get something from Fenby with which to satisfy his own curiosity. But in this he was doomed to disappointment, for Fenby was never communicative and certainly was not yet ready, even if he were ever willing, to talk the situation over with anyone.

Nevertheless Ley tried. He and Miss Knox Forster happened to be in the hall when Fenby came back, and he at once started the conversation by saying that they had found out what was wrong with Cargate's car.

"Something," he said, "had got stuck in the exhaust."

"What was it?" Miss Knox Forster put in. "I wish I had thought of that. It started to go wrong when I fetched Mr. Macpherson from Larkingfield and I only just got back from taking him to the station. It nearly died on me on the drive. I spent most of the afternoon trying to put it right, but I never thought of looking at the exhaust."

It sounded unimportant to Fenby, but it did answer the question of how she had spent that afternoon. Yet it was unusual, and by long habit Fenby never overlooked any departure from the common routine. Consequently he listened while Ley babbled on.

"Somehow or another a bit of cotton waste had got sucked up and jammed in it. Directly I got the exhaust clear the car was in perfectly good order. If only Cargate had known, he need not have gone by train at all."

At that Miss Knox Forster shivered.

"He drove very fast, you know. Supposing that his heart had failed while he was driving? The car might have gone anywhere. If it had been in a town, for instance, he might have killed any number of people."

It was on the tip of Fenby's tongue to ask whether Cargate ever took snuff while he was driving. It sounded a little unlikely that he would, but he remembered in time that not everyone knew, or was supposed to know, how close was the relationship between Cargate's snuff and his death. Instead, he asked what was the reason for the journey to town on that day.

"I don't know, for certain," Miss Knox Forster answered, "except that he said he might possibly go and see you, Mr. Ley, if you were in. Yes, I know that he didn't arrange an appointment—I think he hadn't made up his mind. It was only a subsidiary point. The main thing, I believe, was something to do with his stamp collection. I think that Mr. Macpherson had told him that some of them were forgeries and he was going to find out some other expert to tell him about them. I think that he no longer quite trusted Macpherson. Or perhaps he just wanted a second opinion."

"Did he take them with him?"

"No. I don't think that he had got that far. He was only going to find out an expert and get him to come here. They're rather bulky. He never liked letting them out of his hand. I think that he had a fear they might be stolen and besides they are very easily damaged. But I'm afraid that I don't know very much about it, because I always thought that it was a peculiarly silly hobby."

"I suppose that some time I shall have to sell them and I haven't the faintest notion how to do it," Ley put in.

"Public auction," Fenby suggested. "And if any of them are forgeries, the auctioneer will probably tell you quickly enough."

"With books and pictures, yes; but I wonder if that is equally true of stamps? I don't happen to have had a philatelist client before. Still, there's no hurry."

"No," Fenby agreed. As soon as he got Ley alone he intended to warn him against any precipitate action. Somehow he felt that there might be something yet to be discovered in one of the stamp albums. Then he turned to Miss Knox Forster and asked her if she happened to know of anyone other than Macpherson with whom Cargate had had dealings concerned with stamps.

"Plenty of people," was the answer, "but I don't know which are experts. I'll look up the addresses for you straight-away."

"I wish you would. It may save me trouble."

"No time like the present." She turned with character-istic efficiency towards her own sitting-room to obtain the information at once. "Oh, by the way," she said, "I suppose you don't mind my throwing these roses away? They're nearly dead now."

Fenby looked at them dully. There was something about them that he knew that he had intended to find out, but he had had a long day and he could not remember what it was. The length of the silence became so absurd that even Ley stared at the bowl. Eventually Fenby pulled himself together with a jerk.

"The roses? Oh, I'm sorry, I was day-dreaming. By all means throw them away. They never last, do they?"

"The table will look bare without any flowers on it, won't it?" Ley of course had to say something and Fenby found his opinion of the solicitor going down, but Miss Knox Forster was always agreeable, perhaps even consciously agreeable to an irritating degree, and, with the comment that perhaps they would last till the next morning, she went off to get the addresses which she had just been going to fetch.

"Do you mind handing that stamp collection over to me?" Fenby asked while she was away.

Ley thought a minute.

"I'm afraid I do. You see I am responsible for his prop-erty—to the nation apparently."

"And I might steal it?" Fenby for once lacked his usual urbanity.

"No, but it is not the proper thing to do. I'm speaking

professionally. Besides, if there are any forgeries in it, it might be awkward for you. I mean somebody might say that it was you who substituted them."

Fenby sighed. It sounded silly and he was quite willing to take the risk, but when a lawyer said that he was speaking professionally, he knew from past experience that to reason with him was a waste of time. All the same when, later on, he had interviewed Macpherson, it proved a slight nuisance because, though it was not vital to his case, he did want to know exactly what was the state of that sixpenny St. Vincent of a distinctive deep yellow-green colour, which had for a few moments been lying with its gum touching the mixture of snuff and (perhaps) potassium cyanide. It had, so Macpherson said, been remounted. Indeed, but for the chance that it had been the mount, not the stamp, which Macpherson had licked, a different person might have met his death and straightaway instead of the next morning. The procedure of sticking it in again might have removed all traces of any extraneous substance which might have adhered to the back of the stamp, but perhaps there was still some. You did not, Fenby remembered, put a stamp mount over the whole of the back of the stamp.

"I had hoped," Blayton began nervously to approach the (to him) tiresome subject of stamp collecting, "to have relieved the Court of the necessity of considering the events of that day not only after five o'clock, but after an even earlier hour. For it is admitted that at about 3.45 a particular stamp was placed for a while in the snuffbox—an odd receptacle for it, but I will explain later how that arose—and after some difficulty that actual stamp was obtained and submitted to some extent to analysis.

"It was not an easy matter, since it was a sixpenny stamp

issued by the island of St. Vincent and there were several of these, at least a dozen I am informed, in Henry Cargate's collection which, to those of us who are not stamp collectors, would all look identically the same, or very nearly so. But to the trained philatelist who delights in minutiæ, there are differences, so that some are worth a few shillings and some a considerable number of pounds.

"This particular one happened by an evil chance to be the most valuable of all. Indeed I am informed that if you were to go into the shop of the dealers who issue what is perhaps the generally accepted standard British catalogue, they would ask you to pay one hundred and ten pounds for it. It was possible, therefore to identify this particular specimen, but a stamp is a brittle thing and Mr. Ley, as Henry Cargate's executor and in a sense as trustee for the nation owing to the peculiarities of the will which he had to administer, was naturally anxious—rightly, if I may say so—to see that this valuable property was not damaged, for he was told, and those who gave the opinion still adhere to it, that if any of the gum was removed from the back of the stamp, or the slightest thinning took place in the paper on which it was printed, that then the value of that stamp would be depreciated, not slightly, but by fifty per cent, or even seventy-five per cent, or perhaps by even more than that, even though the surface, which would to you and me appear to be all that was of moment, was undamaged. I find it hard to believe, but I am universally informed that that is true."

Blayton paused to let this sink in and then went on:

"I tell you that simply to explain why Mr. Ley could not allow, from a professional point of view, so exhaustive an examination of that stamp as he would otherwise have granted, unless very strong reasons were given to him why this hundred and ten pound piece of paper should be damaged. And at the time it was not possible to provide him with those reasons.

"Nor subsequently, I will admit, has it proved to be absolutely vital that that stamp should have been examined more closely. Had it been possible, we should have known definitely and certainly that the potassium cyanide had been blended with the snuff before 3.45, and it is part of my case that it was done by that hour, but since I can prove that it was not possible that it could be done after 5 p.m. I am not distressed that that examination could not be exhaustively performed.

"Nevertheless, Mr. Ley did, though with reluctance, allow some processes to be carried out and in particular the mount, the small piece of transparent, adhesive paper which was used to affix the stamp to the album, was exhaustively examined. The analyst who carried out that test, will tell you that in his opinion there was the veriest shade of a trace of potassium cyanide on it. If that is so, and though he cannot be quite certain of it, he will tell you that it is highly probable, we need not worry to consider what happened after 3.45 p.m.

"So then, gentlemen of the jury, we have those four periods, the few minutes around a quarter past eleven, in the morning, a further few from 11.30 to, say, 11.38, the long period between noon and a quarter to two, of which as I have explained to you only the five minutes directly after one o'clock and the five minutes before 1.45 are of importance; and fourthly we have the hour of half-past three.

"And corresponding roughly with those four periods, but not exactly, are four people."

Part III
Analysis

Fenby was both a conscientious and a methodical man, and he very often found that to put things down on paper was of considerable assistance in helping to clear his brain.

Certainly the case of Henry Cargate was one which was likely to benefit by being treated on those lines for it must resolve itself into a question of detail, perhaps of contradiction, certainly of analysis.

Accordingly, he got out his scribbling-pad and put headings to a number of slips of paper. Then he went carefully through all the statements which had been made to him and put each of them into its relevant place. It was a tribute to his tact that everyone concerned had been quite gladly prepared to sign a document which omitted nothing that had been in Fenby's notes and which he had considered to have any possibility of being relevant.

"Position of snuffbox," was his first heading. Gradually the paper filled up with such information as he had about it, noting the approximate time and the informant in each case. In the end it ran as follows:

9.45   Being cleaned by Raikes.

10.0	Put on table at Cargate's left hand—Raikes.
10.0	Put on table at Cargate's right hand—Miss Knox Forster.
10.45	or soon after—on table on left-hand side—(Cargate drew his attention to it)—Yockleton.
11.30	Picked up by Cargate—Yockleton.
2.30	On table. Initials right way up to anyone sitting at desk—Macpherson.
3.30	On table. Initials reverse way up to any one sitting at desk—Macpherson.
3.30	Picked up by Cargate. Stamp found inside it—Macpherson.

The entries for ten o'clock involved a small contradiction by Miss Knox Forster or Raikes—probably the former—but it might well be that it had been moved and put back again. Fenby left the point and examined his second sheet.

"Position of Bottle."

July 11th—bought in Great Barwick.

Note. No information as yet obtained as to position until next morning, but whoever put the potassium cyanide into the snuff did so after 9.45 a.m. on July 12th. Since, however, the poison was bought previously this earlier period may have to be examined if the subsequent ones all prove blank.

10.45	On table. Letter put on it when Yockleton arrived. Presumably resting against it is meant. Cargate said to have mentioned this by Raikes, and to have complained of letter being moved.

10.45   Or soon after—on table. Cargate referred to it being quite close to snuffbox. (Yockleton's account of interview with Cargate.)

11.30   Or just before—on window-sill when went to fetch rose from bed outside— Miss Knox Forster.

11.30   On window-sill when returned from seeing vicar off. Label facing him, Cargate, as reported by Raikes.

11.39   (about) Cargate turns bottle round— Raikes.

12.0   On window-sill. Label towards window— Hardy Hall.

3.30   Right-hand side of window-sill. Label towards window—Macpherson.

5.0   Window-sill. Label towards window— Hardy Hall again.

Fenby whistled gently. Had somebody really been as hurried as all that? Or as incredibly careless? Had somebody been over-confident that death by heart failure would be certified with examination? He turned to the medical evidence which had now reached him.

Undoubtedly the signs of death were entirely consistent with heart failure just as much as with poisoning by potassium cyanide. If it had not been for the sample of snuff which Dr. Gardiner had obtained, it would have been very hard to have suggested that death had been due to anything but natural causes but with it—well, it would take a good deal of explaining away provided that there was otherwise a fairly convincing case. It occurred to Fenby that his thoughts were wandering and that he must stick to his own job. He hoped that everything else would be as suggestive as the page he had completed, but he could hardly expect that it would.

Sheets 3 and 4 contained a brief statement of the movements of Miss Knox Forster and of Raikes. They were rather meagre sheets, but before he even examined them it caught his attention that there was no sheet at all for Yockleton. Other than the period of his visit to Scotney End Hall, his time was entirely unaccounted for, and the vicarage was within easy walking distance of the hall. Fenby picked up the pad again and headed yet another sheet: "Further Enquiries", under which he wrote: "1. Movements of Yockleton, rest of day," then, though in a rather faint handwriting, to express his own doubts as to whether he would ever do it, he added: "2. Consider if Macpherson could have got from Larkingfield and back again to it earlier in the day." Then he went back to sheets 3 and 4.

The account of Miss Knox Forster's movements was brief and to the point. "9.45. Library. Taking down letters. 10.45. Leaves library. Typing. Doing flowers. 11.30. In hall. Talks to Cargate and Raikes. Flowers. (About) 11.32. Picks rose from bed in front of house. Returns to hall as Raikes goes out. Goes to drawing-room, 11.38. 12, in hall as Cargate returns. 12 noon is summoned by Cargate, and goes with him to garden. 1.0 p.m. goes straight in with him to lunch—no interval. Lunch ends 1.45. Time afterwards unaccounted for except that she picks up Macpherson in Larkingfield and he keeps 2.30 appointment. 3.45. Drives Macpherson off. Spent most of afternoon trying to see why car was out of order."

There were gaps in it but mostly—except perhaps between 11.30 and 11.38—they were at times which were of no importance since Cargate himself had been in the library.

Fenby put it down and returned to the information about Raikes.

There was no doubt about it. There were discrepancies as to the eight minutes during which Cargate and Yockleton were looking at the wasps' nest. Raikes, for instance, had entirely failed to hear Miss Knox Forster go out to get the rose. Of course there was the suggestion that the butler had himself put forward, that any sound she had made had been drowned by the noise of his own movements around the dining-room and in laying the table.

Then again Miss Knox Forster thought that when she returned Raikes had just been going through the door towards the servants' hall, whereas Raikes had said that when he went through that door, Miss Knox Forster was in the drawing-room. Almost certainly as to that, since Miss Knox Forster herself said she had been to the drawing-room, Raikes must be right. Fenby read through his notes again and very soon saw the explanation. What Miss Knox Forster had seen was not Raikes going through the door at the far end of the hall, but the door closing behind Mrs. Perriman, whose call to him Raikes had ignored. That, too, explained why the cook had risked calling to him when Miss Knox Forster might have considered it bad manners. Mrs. Perriman had known what Raikes did not, namely, that Miss Knox Forster was not at that moment in the hall.

That then was settled, and Fenby's examination reached lunch time on July 12th quite happily. For a while his pen hovered. Then he briefly put down on the "Further Enquiries" sheet, the word "washing", as the third item. He added a question mark, and went on to consider how Raikes had spent his afternoon.

To his annoyance, he found that except for the words:

"2.30, announces Macpherson. 4.30, brings tea," he had no real information. Of course he had a good deal of information as to what happened at 4.30, but previous to that he really had nothing. He did not even really know why Raikes had had to announce Macpherson at all when, after all, Miss Knox Forster had brought him up and was presumably capable of taking him to Cargate's library. On the whole he thought it seemed a reasonable guess to imagine that as this was the time when the car had first showed signs of being out of order, she had stayed to try to find out what the defect was, after, probably, contenting herself with passing on the stamp dealer to Raikes. It was a guess, but so likely, that Fenby did not think it worth while putting it down as enquiry number four.

Instead he turned his attention to considering what doubts, if any, existed against all those who might be concerned, and what motive anybody had had for killing Cargate. That it was an excellent thing to have done, everybody except Raikes seemed to unite in agreeing, but it was one thing to think that someone might be better dead, and quite another to decide to murder that somebody. Yet that was exactly what had been done. Or at least so it appeared to Fenby.

To commit a murder because it was A Good Thing. Well, that was a new idea and perhaps not a quite impossible one. Hamlet, for instance, regarded it as a duty, and, if he had killed his uncle, seemed to expect everyone to regard it as a necessary piece of justice. He would probably have been definitely pained at the suggestion that the fact that he would inherit a kingdom was more than a by-product of the act. Again, leaving the world of fiction, there was always Charlotte Corday, and she had invariably been regarded as a heroine. Perhaps, therefore, it was not such a new idea. But Fenby sincerely hoped that it was not going to become a common one. If Charlotte Corday was going at long last to have her imitators in private as well as in public life, it was going to be very tiresome, to say the least of it, to Scotland Yard.

But if it was not something of that class, what could it be? Supposing that someone was not quite so altruistic as he pretended to be? For instance there was Macpherson. It might be possible to work up a theory that he was genuinely anxious to help to preserve the trade of which he was a member. There was no doubt, for instance, that his thoughts were constantly fixed on stamps and that he viewed everything, even the initials on the snuffbox, in terms of stamps. Also it was perfectly true that the existence of a forger of any appreciable skill was a real danger to all collectors and dealers. It might be that he felt that so strongly that he regarded anyone whom he knew to be one, as a venomous snake to be extirpated at the earliest possible opportunity.

But that begged a number of questions. First, was Cargate a forger at all—or was he a dupe? If he was dishonest, was Macpherson really unable to prove it? Because to demonstrate it publicly would be to draw the snake's fangs in part; but only in part, since though every stamp that emanated from him would be suspect by those who knew, there would often be a suspicion that the innocent might be unintentional intermediaries. Still to justify so drastic an action as murder, it seemed necessary to assume that there was an intermediate state when Macpherson was morally certain but had no proof that he could publish to the world.

That was possible, but it was equally conceivable that an exactly opposite state of affairs existed, and that the forger was not Cargate but Macpherson himself. In that case the presence of forgeries in Cargate's collection was easily accounted for. They would have been supplied by Macpherson, and

Fenby remembered that Cargate had in fact implied such a thing with regard to the no-accent variety of the block of Irish ten shillings.

Fenby began to consider the points in Macpherson's story which struck him as being doubtful. He had first of all had an undoubted opportunity though a very short one. He knew quite a remarkable amount about the position of the snuffbox and the bottle, neither of which in the least concerned him. He had even commented on the weight of the snuffbox. Then, when Cargate had accused him of stealing the stamp, he had been far too willing to be searched; he knew where the sixpenny St. Vincent had got to, and he carefully avoided licking it himself. Perhaps too much weight ought not to be attached to that last point, since to moisten the mount was, after all, the usual method. All the same, the fact remained.

Then he wanted to buy Cargate's collection. Fenby could well believe that if it was full of forgeries which could in any way be traced to Macpherson himself—and the possibility of tracing individual stamps Fenby had gathered, though very difficult, was not always absolutely out of the question in the case of items of extreme and unusual variety—then it would be essential for him to get the collection back into his hands. Finally Fenby remembered that Macpherson seemed to have known that the box contained snuff without having ever had any legitimate opportunity of obtaining that knowledge, and, lastly, there was that rather grim remark of Cargate's that he was "lucky still to have the box".

Yes, Macpherson could not be ruled out. But was he the type of man who would commit a murder?

On the whole Fenby thought that he was. He was impetuous, quick to take offence, a fanatic in the excessive interest which he took in his business; he had a mind sufficiently quick and alert to have conceived the plan, and ruthless enough to have executed it, and though the two possible sets of motives could not be both concurrently in being, either of them would be a powerful incentive to him.

But it was not fair to concentrate upon him alone. For instance, if it was suspicious that Macpherson was ready to be searched, it might just as well be said that it was even more suspicious that Yockleton had refused to be; and if Macpherson had wanted to defend the stamp trade, or himself, the vicar equally wanted to protect the village and its corporeal and spiritual needs. Moreover, there was again the same alternative. Supposing that he had in fact attempted to steal the emerald? Supposing that his account of what Cargate had said to him was coloured so as to represent Cargate's action as that of attempting to plant the emerald on him, whereas in fact it had been to recover the stone without too great a scandal? Yockleton had said that everyone knew that he was the last person who would ever do such a thing and that, therefore, he could face the accusation with equanimity, but supposing that they knew nothing of the kind? Again, it was equally true that anyone in his position ought never to allow himself to be suspected, and that an accusation was almost as bad as a proof.

He too had had his opportunity, and had also been peculiarly aware of the position of the snuffbox and the poison. For instance, in the case of the bottle, it was undoubtedly on the table when he arrived and it was equally certainly on the window-sill soon after he left, and moreover it must have been moved about that time, because when Cargate returned at 11.38, it was in a position which caught his attention and annoyed him.

Fenby picked up his "further enquiry" sheet, and put down:

"4. Just when was bottle removed from table to window-sill and by whom?"

As he wrote the words, the face of the vicar, bald and blue-eyed, seemed to be before him. Undoubtedly a man of strong personality and quick brain, and moreover perfectly prepared to make a martyr of himself if he considered the cause sufficiently good. Besides it had not escaped Fenby's attention that there was evidently something on Yockleton's conscience. He seemed to be glad that Cargate was dead, but ashamed to be so. "As," thought Fenby, "he ought. But you never know quite where you are with these religious chaps. They mix up doing what is right with reaching the right end, or is that confined to the Jesuits and such-like only?"

A moment's consideration made him realize that when he had to deal with matters of theology he was definitely ignorant. "But anyhow," he went on, "when it comes to a question of snakes, they can be completely ruthless and per-suade themselves that they are right to be so. Though I must confess that if he did do it, from what I have seen of him, he would probably confess it at once with apparent humili-ation but real pride. He's just the stuff of which martyrs are made. Now Miss Knox Forster isn't that sort. She would be quite capable of killing anyone cheerfully in between typing a letter and doing the flowers, but she wouldn't confess to it. She'd cover it up if she could. Efficiently too. And yet I don't know. She gets things done, but she does them in a slapdash way. She's rather in too much of a hurry it seems to me. Those tall, clumsy women are always falling over their own feet metaphorically as well as literally."

If it was going to be an inside job, it had to be Raikes or her so far as he could make out. Now Raikes was the only person who had expressed any regret that Cargate was dead.

It was an upside-down paradoxical business, and perhaps that was a train of thought that he ought to follow up. Was it, for instance, true? Was Raikes really able to treat in so cavalier a fashion the dismissal that he had received? He was not, so Fenby judged by appearances, a young man and it might be very hard for him to get another position, especially if there was any possibility that the emerald had been stolen, and that Raikes was in fact a thief. He had said that he had been given the sack before and he knew all about Cargate's trick of accusing people of stealing things. Supposing that some of those thefts had been real and that they had been committed by Raikes, and that Cargate had forgiven him time after time, and that finally on July 12th he had fallen again and wasted the absolutely last chance that had been given to him? In that case he would go without a character, perhaps even to jail. Was it by any chance in connection with that that Cargate had intended to see Ley on that Friday, July 13th? Or was it in connection with Macpherson? Only Cargate knew, and it was quite useless to try to guess.

Still, Raikes's conduct did look a little different now. He was on the verge of being sacked, and he suspected that he might find himself either in the street without a reference or in prison, whereas, if Cargate were dead, he would still preserve his reputation. He might even have hoped that something was left to him in Cargate's will. People often did reward long service and only Miss Knox Forster and Ley apparently had known Cargate's odd testamentary dispositions.

They were peculiar enough. Even the will was couched in terms of sarcasm, Fenby now knew. Cargate had apparently expressed a wish that his carefully acquired money should be spent on something perfectly useless; he had indicated subways as an example, because, as he expressed it, "nobody can ever be induced to use them, and, therefore, they do no good to anyone except the man who has to clean them".

On that Fenby seemed to see Miss Knox Forster shaking her head with a puzzled expression and saying that it was entirely beyond her; she, at any rate, seemed to think that Cargate's money was going to be useful for the first time in its existence.

Just for a moment a wild idea flitted through Fenby's mind. Was it absolutely certain that Cargate had not committed suicide just in order to be a nuisance? It really seemed as if a man capable of such odd economic theories might even have done that, especially if he thought that his heart was even worse than it was or if he was suffering from a fit of depression due to realizing how justly unpopular he was.

Really the more Fenby thought of it the harder it was to exclude so grotesque a possibility. Nobody could more easily have added the crystals to the snuff. Nobody was more likely to have adopted in grim humour so inconvenient a place and so irritating a time when suspicion could fall on several people. But if it was done to annoy, it ruled out the fit of depression or fear of a heart attack since Cargate would have been in no mood to joke and with that, all possible motive for causing his own death vanished.

Besides, now that Fenby thought about it again, not even Cargate was capable of regarding his own death as an ironic piece of humour; for one thing he would not be able to be present to appreciate it. And for another he would have placed himself on the level of a nest of wasps—and he would never have done that. No, on the whole, the wild possibility could safely be left out.

But all this was getting far away from the point and, with a jerk, Fenby brought himself back to the details before him.

He looked at the amount of time available for Macpherson, for Yockleton, for Miss Knox Forster, and for Raikes, to take the potassium cyanide crystals out of the bottle and mix them with the snuff. The very mention of the word "crystals" brought back to his mind an idea which had been in the back of it all the time, and which he had forgotten to investigate fully. Those crystals were too large to be put in the snuff just as they were. They must have been broken up or pounded in some way or another, so that primarily they would not be obvious and secondly they would be more readily absorbed in the mucous membrane and so act more efficiently and rapidly.

So far, though he had searched, there had been no signs of anything in the library in which such a process had definitely taken place, but there was nothing conclusive in that. It might have been done, for instance, in an ash-tray with the stopper of the bottle, and the contents quickly put into the snuffbox and the ash-tray dusted or—nasty thought—put in the pocket of *a man who would not consent to be searched.*

It was a very long shot, and Fenby disliked long shots. Nevertheless, he wrote down: "Is there an ash-tray or anything of that sort missing?"

But, to be fair, he had to admit, though only to himself, that he had not given sufficient thought to this question of the grinding-down of the crystals. It did undoubtedly give both Yockleton and Macpherson very little time indeed in which to act. Also it made into almost certainly too short a period the minute and a half during which, with Miss Knox Forster picking her rose in the garden or looking at the flowers in the drawing-room, Raikes had the library available to himself alone. Unless—and this was an idea—he had taken the crystals while she was in the garden, ground them down in the dining-room and slipped back when he knew Miss Knox Forster was in the drawing-room. Of course then that was the reason why he could not have answered Mrs. Perriman when she called to him, because his voice would have come, not from the dining-room but from the library! That, too, would be why he would not admit that he had heard Miss Knox Forster go out, and the great hurry that he was in would account for the really colossal blunder that he had made, namely that he had put the bottle down on the window-sill instead of on the table. For there was no doubt that it had been moved at that time. Fenby stopped suddenly. It might just as well have been moved by Yockleton a little earlier in similar circumstances.

Moreover, now he came to think of it, to go into the library at all, was a frightful risk for Raikes to run because Miss Knox Forster was just outside the window and she might very well have seen him. Also he could not possibly have known that she would go into the drawing-room afterwards.

But perhaps though the potassium cyanide was taken from the bottle at that time, it was not put into the snuff until much later? Was there really no moment when Raikes could have got to the library for a minute or two between twelve and one-forty-five? Fenby looked through his notes carefully. Just for a minute he hoped that he had found a discrepancy, for Miss Knox Forster happened to mention that she and Cargate had gone straight into lunch from the garden—she had rather resented the fact on the grounds of normal cleanliness—but Raikes had said that they had settled down to lunch in "just the ordinary time", which seemed to imply something longer than a direct walk from lawn to dining-room. It was a very tiny point and not even really substantiated as a discrepancy; nevertheless Fenby marked it off as number six of his points for enquiry. Then he nearly crossed it out again. Mrs. Perriman's statements as to the soundness of Raikes's alibi at that period would be very hard to break down.

Still the point must remain as a detail that was wrong. It might be the small detail for which he was looking and which would eventually enable him to find out why Henry Cargate had died in the train. In the train? That reminded him. That exhaust pipe getting stuffed up had seemed to him peculiar. Was it just possible that it was choked on purpose? Perhaps by someone who very much disliked the idea of a dead man at the wheel of a fast-going vehicle since, as Miss Knox Forster had said, that might involve risk to third parties who were quite unconnected with Cargate or anyone who knew him. He must get a little expert advice on the point. Down it went as point number seven.

Then suddenly an idea occurred to him and he looked with feverish excitement through all the analysis that he had made. If just one remark made to him by the person who had caused Cargate's death was a lie, then it allowed everything else to fit into place and he thought that he had got the explanation of everything and that, moreover, he would, with a little good fortune, be able to prove it.

To his list of enquiries he added the words: "8. Roses? 9. Bowl really scratched?" If he got to those questions the answers that he expected, and if his other points, especially the sixth, worked out as he was confident that they would, then he would know. As to that sixth point, though, he noticed that a second lie was necessary, but by the same person, all of whose evidence now he was beginning to suspect. He must get back to Scotney End as fast as he could, and this time he would not content himself with taking written statements.

"For those reasons, members of the jury" (for the answers to Fenby's questions had been as he anticipated and Blayton had explained them carefully in their right place), "the prosecution ask for your verdict against the accused."

"I don't think that they will get mine," thought Ellis to himself. "All the same it depends on the evidence, and if they put the accused in the box a good deal will depend on that. But I think that if I was counsel for the defence—" Then he looked at his fellow jurymen. Judging by their expressions, they were nine-tenths convinced already. Was it fair he wondered, to the accused, to allow the prosecution to put their case first? In these superficial days, was it not possible that the preconceived opinion was even stronger than the last word?

Mr. Justice Smith took the opportunity to adjourn the Court. The opening speech had been to his mind long, rather too long, and he was not sure that it was wise to have dealt with hypothetical lines of defence so early on. But it had been eminently fair, and on the whole he had to admit that, though he had taken a personal dislike to Anstruther Blayton's rather pompous, fussy methods, it had been a clear and convincing bit of work. If Blayton ever succeeded to the Bench—a by no means improbable event—he thought that he would make a good Judge. Perhaps a better Judge than counsel.

Part IV
Defence

"We are going to take a lot of trouble about this case," Vernon pulled a pipe out of his pocket and addressed his junior; "not only on general principles, but because from what you've told me, it's a damned shame that anyone should be hanged for murdering a verminous bit of work like Cargate. It was done with the most excellent intentions and, if you ask my quite unofficial opinion, plenty of people richly deserve to be murdered nowadays and far too few of them actually get bumped off. Consequently we shall fight every point. And I rather think that we ought to win. Really our chief trouble is going to be our actual client. Far too transparently honest for my liking, and just the sort of person who would confess to the crime in the box out of pure mental honesty."

Oliver grinned. He knew the strong, if eccentric character of his leader. It was exactly like Vernon to talk of people deserving to be murdered. In reality he would never hurt anyone in the slightest degree. "We shall have to chance it, I suppose," he said. "It creates a lot of prejudice if you don't put the accused in the box. And I don't think that you need be afraid of too much honesty. If innocent, as we think, so much the better, but if, after all, the prosecution's story is right, there have been two hearty lies already. In fact the trouble is that they are almost proved."

A grunt from Vernon dismissed the point. "Probably be able to get round it. Anyhow we are putting the cart before the horse. We've got lots of time before the trial to think out our defence. What's it going to be?"

"I was going to suggest," Oliver began a little tentatively, since he really felt that questions of policy were his leader's province, "that we might begin by suggesting that he wasn't murdered at all."

"You mean suicide?"

"No. I did think of that, but there isn't any motive for it. At least not fit to bring forward. I meant quite simply that it was not a murder at all."

"You mean that it really was heart failure all the time? I don't remember that being taken as a line before."

"Yes. The medical evidence isn't a bit strong. The post-mortem didn't reveal a single sign that wasn't quite consistent with heart failure. I'm told that it wouldn't anyway because the action of potassium cyanide is in fact to produce heart failure. Then while it is true that the snuff was doped—"

"No chance of getting round that?"

"None whatever, I'm afraid—there is very little evidence that he ever took the snuff. He was just going to do so on the station platform when the porter knocked it off his thumb. Then he gets into the train and, according to this man Hardy the baker, he was just going to do so again. Now Hardy had seen him thinking of doing so on the platform. Couldn't we suggest that Hardy imagined the rest?"

"We can suggest anything that we like, but I fancy that Hardy's answer will be that his curiosity was aroused and that was why he was watching. I think that any question about that might prove to be a boomerang."

"Well, then, what about saying that though he was seen to be just about to take a pinch, he never actually did. That in fact he died of natural causes just before?"

"I see that the prosecution," Vernon turned over the papers before him, "are going to get Hardy to say that he saw a flush come over Cargate's cheeks just as he died. I don't know, but I imagine that, if they think that is worth while putting in, that it is in some way a sign of having taken this particular poison."

"I believe that it is, but I think that we could get round that. You see Hardy only saw his face reflected in the window. I believe that if we cross-examined him about what else he saw, that he would get into a muddle and so we could discount that."

"Very well, then. I shall take that in hand, but I don't honestly think that it is going to do us much good. It's too great a coincidence that a man should die of heart failure when he is within a split second of taking something which would have killed him."

"Coincidences have happened, and it's up to the prosecution to prove that they haven't again. If you come to think of it, I must say that I didn't know that to sniff up anything of that sort was a fatal thing to do. I remember smelling as a small boy one of those bottles into which one put unfortunate butterflies and it didn't kill me. But it did give me a headache though," he added reflectively.

"Exactly. And it did kill the butterfly. Also you only sniffed it. You didn't put some of it in carefully ground powder right up your nose and you didn't have a weak heart. No, I don't think that that line is much good—anyhow it only removes us from murder to attempted murder, because you can't get round the fact that the crystals were ground up—but that doesn't mean that we won't try it. Only we must think out other lines as well. Who is trying it by the way?"

"Smith probably."

"Then I don't think we shall have any luck, but we can try."

Vernon's long experience had enabled him to form a picture of what would happen that proved to be substantially accurate. At the close of the case for the prosecution, he rose and put a preliminary point. "I submit, my lord, that the prosecution have not proved that the deceased was ever murdered at all, and on that ground I ask your lordship to withdraw the case from the jury."

Mr. Justice Smith looked startled, as well he might, but he was a man who at all times liked to mix his law with as much spice of originality as might well be permitted. A subtle and original point that was not too obvious was certain to appeal to him and he would allow his fancy to toy with it and caress it, as a cat would play with a mouse. But, like the cat, he very seldom let the mouse escape, and so, although he was delighted to listen to the suggestion that Vernon was putting forward (though it had originally taken shape in Oliver's brain), his common sense never really allowed him to consider that there was any substance in it. Nevertheless he listened with pleasure to what Vernon had to say.

Then he looked at his notes. "I see, Mr. Vernon," he said, "that the witness, Hardy or Baker—there appears to be some confusion as to his surname—spoke of seeing the box with the sparkling lid appear from the deceased's pocket, and the light brown powder being put on his left thumb. A lot of it there was, so the witness said, and he added that he admired the skill with which it was kept in place. Then he says that the thumb travelled surely up to Cargate's nose, and with a powerful sniff the brown powder disappeared."

"Yes, my lord, but you will remember that I cross-examined him about it."

"You did. Let me see. 'You were, when the deceased took the pinch of snuff sitting in your compartment.' No, it was before that. If I remember aright, you called the attention of the Court twice to the fact that the witness was only in the corridor. Ah, here we are. Let me read it to you." His lordship adjusted his spectacles, and read aloud.

"'You saw this compound placed on the deceased's thumb?'

"'Yes.'

"'You had seen that done before? Are you sure that the one incident did not remind you of the other?'

"'It made me want to look.'

"'Exactly. You wanted to see what happened. Did you get a very good view? It isn't very easy to see something which is only reflected, is it?'

"'Not so good a view as I should have liked, but I saw well enough.'

"'You saw the powder on his thumb?'

"'I did.'

"'And then you saw that it had disappeared?'

"'Yes.'

"'It might have fallen on to the floor?'

"'He raised his thumb to his nose.'

"'And then he sneezed.'

"'He did. Right violently.'

"'I suggest to you that the sneeze blew the powder off his thumb.'

"'It might have done, but I think that he sniffed it up.'

"'But he might not?'"

"'Well, he *might* not.'

"I remember, Mr. Vernon," Mr. Justice Smith put down his notes, "thinking that the witness expressed by the intonation of his voice, extreme doubt as to that."

"But he had to admit that he might have blown it on to the floor."

"He did indeed. Still—" There was very little doubt what Mr. Justice Smith thought of it. "I see," he said, "that you then went on to deal with the question of the alleged flush on Mr. Cargate's cheek. You will probably, however, agree with me that though the witness was a little doubtful as to such matters as the colour of the deceased's tie, he was not really shaken on that point. Moreover, in reply to Mr. Blayton, he said that he saw quite clearly that the snuff placed on Mr. Cargate's thumb actually disappeared up his nostril. What have you to say to that?"

"That the witness was jumping to conclusions. I am not impugning his honesty—merely his accuracy. I put, as you have just mentioned, my lord, various questions to him as to Mr. Cargate's dress and movements, and he was unable to answer them. His recollection is very faint on all points except when we come to those which are really important, and there he is strangely certain and precise."

Mr. Justice Smith considered the matter. It might well have been said in reply that the witness was in fact confident; that he noticed the points that were essential because they were the points that were interesting and that he did not waste his time in looking at those details which were irrelevant; and that moreover there was no doubt but that the snuff was poisoned.

Out of the corner of his eye Sir Trefusis saw Blayton starting to rise and he did not feel that he wanted to hear him any more. "I don't think that I need trouble you, Mr. Blayton. I see no reason for withdrawing the case from the jury. But I shall remind them that they will have to satisfy themselves that Henry Cargate did in fact die as the result of absorbing potassium cyanide through his mucous membrane. Go on, Mr. Vernon."

"If that succeeds," Vernon brought his thoughts back from considering what might happen, and continued his conference with his junior, "well and good, but naturally we must not assume that it will. The next point is that it seems to me that there is an elementary flaw in what I take to be the prosecution's whole case. It seems too good to be true, but don't they assume all the way through that, because the poison was put into the snuff after 9.45 a.m. on the 12th, that it must have been taken out of the bottle after that time? Why shouldn't it have been taken out before, ground down at leisure, and put in later?"

"I think that they very nearly did fall into the trap. If you will look at my cross-examination at the police court and at the depositions we have got about that, you will see how nearly they did. But Fenby (he was the detective in charge), spotted it in the end, and as bad luck for us would have it, he was able to cover it completely. Look at what Raikes said then." Oliver produced two more documents, and pointing to a passage, read it through quickly.

"'Mr. Cargate purchased a quantity of potassium cyanide in Great Barwick on the afternoon of July 11th. He told me so himself. He did not get back in time to give it to Hardy the gardener that night. On the morning of July 12th, in my presence and in that of Miss Knox Forster, he unlocked a drawer in his writing-desk and put the bottle on the table, saying that he was going to tell Hardy to use it that evening and that he would give him some instructions during the day about its use. I had been summoned to the room to receive directions as to cleaning the box which Mr. Cargate used for keeping snuff in.' That, I am afraid, means that it could not be got at. Moreover, Miss Knox Forster confirms what Raikes says."

"Unless someone had a duplicate key."

"A Yale lock, and there is not the slightest evidence of a duplicate or of Cargate's keys being missing at any time. He kept them locked up in a safe at night which required a special combination in order to open it. He was a suspicious man, as it happens, and took rather a lot of precautions."

"And there isn't anything to suggest tampering with the safe or the drawer?"

"Nothing at all, I'm afraid."

"Then that goes by the board. But I shall bear it in mind in case an opportunity occurs. It seems to me that our strongest points are the weakness of the motive, the possibility of it being one of three other people, and, generally speaking, the lack of very convincing proof. We shall be able all the way through to throw doubts on the accuracy of the witnesses and of the certitude of the conclusions that the prosecution are drawing."

"Are we going to put forward an alternative theory?"

Vernon thought for a minute. "On the whole I think not. If one does it without really strong grounds, it rather puts the jury's back up. But I think that we may say that though we do not suggest it as a fact, nevertheless we would like to point out that it was just as possible for A to have done it as B. For instance this stamp dealer—what's his name?"

"Macpherson."

"Macpherson, Macpherson," Vernon repeated it twice to

get it into his head. "It's pretty clear that he had nothing to do with it, but Blayton will have to deal with the point that he did have half a chance, because *all* the time must be covered. It will come out that Cargate was a rogue and composed stamps from portions of others—very likely Blayton will produce those half-prepared West Indian things that Fenby found and the apparatus and inks for putting on or removing parts of surcharges and overprints. If we are lucky, he will get tied up in technicalities and begin boring everyone. He may even rather stress the point because he has got to suggest that Cargate was such a wrong 'un that to get rid of him was a public-spirited action. It was of course entirely meritorious and that in itself may rather prejudice the jury in our favour. Still, that's beside the point. Where was I?"

"You were talking about Macpherson."

"Oh yes. Now is there any reason for being certain that he did *not* do it?"

"He was able to prove that he was never nearer to Scotney End Hall than Larkingfield on the morning of the 12th. Consequently it could not have been he who moved the bottle in the morning. Also he had, according to his own story which seems to be borne out by his action in going on selling stamps to and buying them from Cargate, no absolutely clear idea that there was anything wrong about Cargate until that afternoon—and then he says that he was doubtful. In fact he went down to answer some accusations of Cargate's, and he's got the letter showing them."

"He might have started suspecting then—or at any rate getting annoyed."

"He might, but his demeanour was perfectly friendly, as Raikes has said, when he was shown in, and in the car coming up he spoke to Miss Knox Forster about what a good customer Cargate was."

"Bluff perhaps?"

"It might be, but he could not have expected to find not only some poison ready at hand but, in addition, the means of administering it in an unusual way. It would not occur to everyone that it was lethal at all. And he had something like three minutes in which to decide that it was, make up his mind, not only how he would do it, but that he would do it at all, pound the crystals into powder—incidentally finding something with which that could be done—and mix the result thoroughly with the snuff. All that when at any moment he might find that Cargate had returned, and Cargate, though the full quarrel was to come later and the accusation of stealing the stamp had not then been made, had implied that there was something funny about the stamps Macpherson had been selling to him. Macpherson knew that Cargate was a suspicious man and he would not have run risks. For instance, if Cargate had returned while he was pounding up the crystals, he could not possibly have explained it away. But, anyhow, I don't think that it could have been done in the time. Moreover, supposing that he had, it would have been done in such a hurry that you would have thought that he would have left some traces. And so far as I know, he didn't."

"What sort of traces do you mean?"

"Well, the bottle, for instance. You notice that the gardener says that at five o'clock it was in exactly the same position as it was at twelve."

"He can't really be sure of that, can he?"

"I don't see how he really can be, but he says he is."

Vernon put down a note. "We might be able to shake him about that, or at any rate to make the jury see that he was swearing to something which was more than any human being could know."

"Yes, I see, but all the same there isn't any positive sign. And unfortunately there are several actual pieces of evidence which, though small in themselves, point against our client. And cumulatively they do add up to an unpleasantly effective whole."

"They do, and we've got to try to deal with them. But I want first of all just to finish with one other possibility. That is Yockleton. Just the sort of chap who would do a murder for the very best of reasons."

"I believe," Oliver laughed, "that he would have been more likely to have done it if Cargate had not suggested that he stole that emerald. After that it might have been thought that he did it to shield himself, and Yockleton might be prepared to murder someone in a good cause and to take the consequences of doing so, but he would never have done it if there was a possibility of his motives being misinterpreted. Besides from what I can hear of him, if he had done it, he would immediately have confessed to it at the first opportunity."

"I wonder," Vernon said. "When it comes to the point people are rather more shy of confessing to crimes which they have really done than you might think—even people of Yockleton's type, whose conscience and sense of duty make them at once the salt of the earth and a perfect nuisance. No, unless you can produce something more definite than that, I shall contemplate uttering the most shameless slanders against Mr. Yockleton."

Oliver thought for a minute before he answered. He liked working with Vernon, who might well have applied to himself the description he had just given of Yockleton. For there was no doubt that there was no one who devoted himself more thoroughly and conscientiously to the cases of his clients than the short, pugnacious, tendentious, but eminently likeable little man who was now insisting on Oliver's answering a case in which neither of them believed. Moreover, it was quite clear to Oliver that he would have to produce a reasonably good answer.

"I think," he began, "that the reasons for excluding Yockleton are rather the same as those for leaving out Macpherson. In the same way that Macpherson has been able to prove that he was not at Scotney End during the morning, so Yockleton has been able to account for all his day after he left Cargate in the morning. And so, as in the case of Macpherson, you have got to assume that he conceived and executed the whole idea while Cargate was fetching the parish magazine."

"In which he had already heaved half a brick at Cargate?"

"Yes. A rather naughty half a brick, because it was criticism by implication instead of being open and direct."

"Very well then. He had the idea in mind when he went there."

"But like Macpherson, he could not have thought it out beforehand, because he could not have known about it."

"He might have heard talk in the village about the wasps' nest. Not a very interesting subject of conversation, but in places like Scotney End they have to make do with what is available."

"But the village and the hall were practically not on speaking terms."

"What about the gardener? He knew some poison was going to be bought?"

"That's true."

"If he did mention it, we might put up the theory that Yockleton planned the whole thing, went and bought some potassium cyanide himself, ground it up before ever he went to see Cargate that morning, himself caused Cargate to go out of the room to fetch something, not necessarily the parish magazine, which is in any case a most improbable thing for Cargate to have read, and while he was away, all he had to do was to slip the powder in. Even so, he was a little slow, and Cargate, coming back suddenly, finds him still fingering the snuffbox, and accuses him of stealing the emerald; or at any rate got the idea of making that accusation."

"Aren't you," Oliver approached the task of throwing doubts on his leader's wisdom with hesitation, "taking rather a lot for granted? I mean, it would be too great a coincidence for Yockleton to have had some potassium cyanide handy, and if he hadn't, where did he get it? It was only the day before, I think only the evening before, that the gardener knew—and by the way, we don't know that he *did* say anything to Yockleton—and according to the register of the chemist at Great Barwick, he sold none except to Cargate. So far as I know, there isn't anywhere else where Yockleton could have got it."

"Those country chemists are sometimes a bit lax about their registers."

"If you don't mind my saying so, the fact that he did record Cargate's purchase rather suggests that Yockleton's would also have been put down if he had made one. And in any case Great Barwick is some distance off, and Yockleton did not have a car."

Vernon sighed. "I'm afraid you're right, but I insist on keeping it in mind. Now look here, what about this as an alternative idea? Suppose that Yockleton arrives in the morning, and while Cargate is fetching this parish magazine, his eye falls on this bottle with its prominent label of 'poison'. 'I wish that I could poison Cargate,' he says to himself. Then he begins playing with fire. He picks up the bottle and turns it over in his hand. 'Might come in handy,' he says, takes an envelope from the writing-table and slips some crystals into it. Then he hears Cargate returning and he hurriedly puts it down again—in the wrong place."

"But he knew that it was on the table. He says that Cargate mentioned it to him, and the whole trouble is that Miss Knox Forster described it as being on the window-sill just before Yockleton left."

"Quite. He put it there."

"But he wouldn't then have said that it was on the table earlier on. Knowing where it was ultimately, as he did, he would have been certain either to have put it back on the table, or to have been careful to say that it was on the window-sill when he arrived."

"Might not that be the mistake he made?"

"It might, I suppose." Oliver did not sound very convinced.

"There you are, then. Then, having got his crystals, Cargate comes back and at once provides him with a spur to his motive by refusing finally to help this other Hardy, Scottish Hardy as he calls him. I agree with you that the accusation about the emerald would be more likely to act as a brake than the other way, but that would not be so about the village. So then Yockleton goes away thoroughly angry and disgruntled, and with the poison, and he thinks out a way of doing it at his leisure. Then, later on, he comes back."

"But he accounted for his day."

"But not for his night."

"Do you mean that he might have broken in during the night? I somehow don't think that Yockleton is a very experienced burglar."

"Cargate thought that he was and perhaps after all he was right!"

"Well, he didn't leave any traces. Moreover, I strongly suspect that that snuffbox was locked up during the night, and that the house was smothered all over with burglar alarms. Cargate would never have been happy without every device of that sort being in operation."

"A competent man like Yockleton would know how to cut them," Vernon laughingly suggested. "No, I suppose that idea is a little too far-fetched."

"Afraid so," Oliver answered. "Besides—I don't know how much Blayton is going to insist on it, because the analyst's report is very undecided, but there is a suggestion that the cyanide was in the snuff as early as 3.45 in any case. There are those very faint traces on the stamp mount. If you ask my opinion, if Blayton puts that forward tentatively, the jury will believe it to be quite true. By the way, it makes another reason why Macpherson's part in the day's events will have to be mentioned."

"I see. Let's hope that Blayton, or his junior, puts it too strongly. Macpherson is just the sort of witness one would hand over to one's junior, and with luck he'll make a mess of it." The grin on Vernon's face let Oliver know that any implication that he might take from that as to his own conduct was in the nature of a leg pull.

"Still," Vernon went on, "that's the merest detail. The result so far is not very helpful. We've got a few small points which we can use in helping to pull the prosecution's case to pieces, and I think that we can make something of them, especially when the other side have to admit that the motive is weak. But the real thing is that in all probability we shall have to agree that it was bound to be either Miss Knox Forster or Raikes. And the Crown, having decided to accuse one of them and bring that person to trial, we shall be at liberty to suggest that it was the other. Or rather, for the reasons that I gave you before as to putting the jury's backs up, confine ourselves to suggesting that it might just as well have been. Now let's get through the evidence as to both of them."

Oliver nodded. "I thought that you would say that. I've got it all analysed here in parallel columns. Really, the hardest thing that we've got to get over is the roses. If only this fellow Ley had not looked at them so hard!"

"Shall we be able to shake him do you think?"

"I doubt it. He's a solicitor and he knows the tricks of the trade."

"Really, really, my dear Mr. Oliver," Vernon pretended to be shocked. "You must not refer to the skilled work of the Bar as 'the tricks of the trade'."

Oliver laughed. "A rose by any other name—" he began. Then he stopped. "I meant that as to 'the tricks of the trade', but of course really it applies even more to the case for the prosecution. Calling the rose by the wrong name is in a way exactly the point, and in a way too it was almost a question of it's not smelling as sweet."

"So I gathered," Vernon answered. "You know, Ley may be a solicitor and therefore a tough nut to crack, but he isn't a gardener and he may get muddled on that."

"He may. But he hasn't so far and honestly I don't think that he will. Besides, more than one person saw those roses, and saw them correctly."

"And if we are to win, we have got to avoid their thorns. Let's see your analysis."

It was a good bit of work, but the more Vernon read it, the less he liked it. Like Fenby, though he was unaware of it, he ended by murmuring: "The roses—and the bowl."

Part V
Summing-Up

Mr. Justice Smith cleared his throat and began his charge to the jury.

"Members of the jury, the accused is charged with the murder of Launcelot Henry Cuthbert Cargate by poisoning him by causing him to take potassium cyanide.

"Some years ago Mr. Justice Avory, in dealing with the case of Jean Pierre Vaquier, quoted these words: "'Of all forms of death by which human nature may be overcome, the most detestable is that of poison, because it can of all others be the least prevented either by manhood or forethought; and therefore in all cases where a man wilfully administers poison to another or lays poison for him and either he or another takes it and is killed by it, the law implies malice although no particular enmity can be proved.'" The learned Judge then went on to say for himself: 'Therefore in this case if you should be driven to the conclusion that the prisoner at the Bar laid this poison for the deceased, intending him to take it, it is not necessary either to search for, much less to establish a motive for his doing so.' With those words, *mutatis mutandis,* I am entirely in agreement.

"Nevertheless, counsel for the prosecution has thought it to be his duty to consider the question of the motives which could have influenced the accused. He summed them up in his closing speech by concentrating upon the character of Henry Cargate, and by pointing out that it was easy to imagine that anyone living in daily touch with him might well have thought that it was a public service to rid the world of such a man. We have seen that Cargate was dishonest in that he forged stamps, and there is a suggestion, though no more than that, that he was a rogue in other similar ways. It has been brought to your attention that he founded his quite considerable fortune by means of activities which were never of direct use to the nation. This is not the proper place to consider what useful function, if any, is performed by the speculator. There is no need for you or me to decide that question. You need only remember that while some people consider that he is almost a necessity, others think that many of the ills of the present world may be laid at his door. It is part of the prosecution's case that the accused took that view.

"Again, it is alleged that Cargate's political outlook was both strong and peculiar, and that these were in great contrast to those of the accused, who thus conceived an antipathy so violent and irrational as to cause to come into existence a desire that Cargate should die. You have heard questions of economics and of disarmament mentioned, and you have had described to you the attitude taken by the deceased towards labour generally and the village of Scotney End in particular. Finally, you have heard that the deceased had made a contemptuous will leaving his property derisively to the nation on the somewhat curious economic ground that he desired to help his fellow men as little as possible during his lifetime, and after his death not at all, and that such a disposition of his property as was proposed would be actually harmful to everybody.

"It is not a theory to which you or I would probably wish to subscribe, but that is of no importance. All that matters is that the accused is stated to have violently disagreed with it. The prosecution's case then is simply this—'in the mind of the accused Cargate alive was a pest, Cargate dead was of value', and that the accused conceived such a hatred for him that when an opportunity arose unexpectedly—and the flames of hatred were fanned by the deceased's treatment of the Rev. Mr. Yockleton—then temptation became too powerful to be resisted, and that Cargate's life was taken in much the same mental attitude and for very similar motives as he himself proposed to destroy the nest of wasps.

"To this the defence offer two lines of thought. In the first place they say that while this might possibly have caused the accused to leave Mr. Cargate's service, it is not sufficient to have caused the crime of murder to have been committed; that such a decisive act was entirely inconsistent with the character of the accused. The prosecution say that it is entirely consistent. I do not think that I can add anything usefully to what has been said to you on that subject, since the procedure of the law of England forces us, for excellent reasons, to form our judgment solely on what we ourselves have observed by the demeanour of the accused in the witness box.

"But the defence are not content with this. They have taken up a second position to which to effect a partial withdrawal, if necessary. This position, however, they have cautiously not put before you in so many words, but nevertheless they have perhaps managed to convey it to your minds. It is, briefly speaking, this. That Cargate was all that the prosecution have implied, and that it was in fact an excellent thing that he has been removed—that his murderer was full of the most excellent intentions. It is a sentimental plea for your sympathy, and I must tell you that if you have formed that idea in your mind, you must dismiss it at once. In the law of England there is such a thing as justifiable homicide, but it has nothing to do with sentiment, and not for one moment does it contemplate that anyone is entitled to say 'So-and-so is better dead. For the sake of the nation at large, I propose to kill him'. Such a proposition is pure nonsense. You have a duty to perform to the public and, as has been said before, whether it be a case of murder, or whether it be a case of petty theft, your duty is the same. You are here to convict the guilty and acquit the innocent, and if you are satisfied that the case is proved, it is your duty to convict because if crime is not detected—I am quoting again from one of my learned brethren—and conviction does not follow detection—crime flourishes.

"So much then for that point. I now want to turn to the suggestion by the defence that Cargate did not meet his death as the result of the presence of the potassium cyanide at all. You have heard the evidence of the witness Hardy, the baker of Scotney End, and it is for you to ask yourselves whether that evidence convinces you that the deceased did in fact take that pinch of snuff. If you decide that he did not, and that his death was purely due to natural causes, then there is an end of the case. That is a question of fact and you have seen the witness Hardy in the box, and you have heard what he has said.

"If you do think that the pinch of snuff was taken in whole or in part, you must next consider the medical evidence. There is no doubt but that Henry Cargate purchased one ounce of potassium cyanide from the chemist in Great

Barwick and brought it away with him in a small glass bottle with a stopper to it. Nor is there any question but that he bought it in order to destroy a wasps' nest. Nor is it disputed that the snuffbox into which it is alleged that this poison was introduced, holds up to approximately half an ounce of a powder of the same specific gravity as snuff.

"You have heard what the analyst attached to the Home Office—an entirely independent witness—has said. He analysed the sample of powder which Dr. Gardiner collected from the floor of the railway carriage at Larkingfield, and found that it consisted of about two-thirds of the type of snuff which had been supplied to Cargate; that there was a certain amount of dust from the floor naturally enough, but that the rest was potassium cyanide. Then you have had the purely medical evidence of two doctors of eminence. They both say that, should a good-sized pinch of snuff have been taken, a grain, or rather more, of potassium cyanide might well have been absorbed through the mucous membrane, and that this would have been sufficient to have caused death, allowing for the state of Henry Cargate's health.

"This medical evidence is not contested by the defence so far. Up to this point they have confined themselves to the question of whether the snuff was ever taken at all. They have suggested that potassium cyanide is an irritating substance, and that the automatic reaction of anyone inadvertently taking it, would be to sneeze it out—would indeed act in exactly the same way as the porter's dog acted when it came into contact with the mixture. But at this point the defence make another suggestion—that even if Cargate did take some of the snuff, he would not have taken a sufficient amount to kill himself unless he had had a weak heart. That in fact Cargate's death was in truth due to his heart. The doctors, as no doubt you noticed, refused to commit themselves too definitely on this point. They were inclined to think that a man in normal health would also have died, but they were *not* positive.

"But really this is an irrelevant point.

"I cannot put the matter better than was done by my learned brother, Mr. Justice Shearman, when he was trying Bywaters and Thompson. Let me read to you what he says: 'If that meant to poison him or to make him die because he was unable to resist it in a heart attack, it is common sense to say that would be murder, just as much as the longest and strongest dose of poison. It is useless to say that because he has got a weak heart, I can give him a smaller dose and then it will be partly from his heart and partly from the dose. A man with a weak heart is entitled to be protected from poison as well as anybody else.' With those remarks I am fully in agreement, and I do not wish to add anything to them. That, I think, is all that I can helpfully say to you on that subject."

As Mr. Justice Smith paused for breath, John Ellis fidgeted uneasily on his hard seat in the jury box. It seemed to him that far too many points were being scored against the defence, compared with those which were mentioned as being in their favour. "May I ask a question, my lord?" he said suddenly.

There was a slight pause which made it clear that his lordship did not entirely approve of such a proceeding. Nevertheless leave to do so was given.

"What importance," Ellis asked, "are we to give to the admission by both doctors that their post-mortem revealed no symptoms of death by poisoning—that death was in fact due to heart failure?"

"Signs, not symptoms, I believe is the correct technical word." It was a mistake which always annoyed Mr. Justice

Smith. Still, he had to admit to himself that to correct it at that juncture was unnecessary pedantry. "The jury will have to decide for themselves how much importance to attach to that point. It is not in dispute between the prosecution and the defence. The prosecution say, 'Death by heart failure and death by poisoning with potassium of cyanide produce the same signs. Therefore the fact that this poison has left no trace, is of no importance. It would not have done so in any case.' The defence say, 'Well and good. But remember that there was no trace.' It will be for you to consider how much importance to attach to those respective points of view. Does that answer your question?"

"Thank you, my lord." Ellis did not think that it did, but he was perfectly certain that it was the only answer that he was going to get.

"Very well, then," Mr. Justice Smith resumed. "We now come to the question as to what happened from the moment when the poison was bought until Cargate administered it to himself, if he ever did so. Much of this is not really in dispute, and I will deal with it quite briefly." With that he recounted how the bottle had been in Cargate's own care until the morning of July 12th, and he brushed aside the possibility of there having been a duplicate key. Even Ellis— who was rapidly developing a strong prejudice against the pale, aquiline face of the Judge—had to agree that in this the evidence had shown that he was perfectly right.

"Down then to the moment when Mr. Yockleton left the library of Scotney End Hall, there is very little dispute as to what happened. It is the next period of eight minutes or so that we have to consider very carefully." Mr. Justice Smith leant forward towards the jury, and in colloquial phraseology, "got down to it".

"This is what the prosecution say.

"They say that during that morning Joan Knox Forster, who is now standing her trial before you, became more and more angry. She was, according to the prosecution, in a highly irritable state already owing to the repeated conflicts on the various matters of opinion to which I have already called your attention, that in fact she regarded him, as I have said, as a pest. Counsel for the Crown permitted himself one or two paradoxes on the subject, that it took a pacifist to have bloodthirsty intentions, and that those who verbally disagree most violently with public war are the most ready to fight in private. You may, or probably you may not, see some force in those remarks, but we are not here to consider the problem in the spirit in which the late Mr. G. K. Chesterton might have considered it in one of his excellent novels. We are here to consider facts, and I think that it would be best if you dismissed those reflections from your minds altogether.

"To continue. The prosecution say then that during the morning of Thursday, July 12th, the accused's anger got out of control and that she decided deliberately to murder her employer. They say that it is possible that at first she only decided to possess herself of the means of doing so and that she did not necessarily decide absolutely to commit the murder at once or even at all. Perhaps she did, perhaps she did not. The prosecution do not pretend to say.

"But they do say that she took steps to get hold of the cyanide of potassium. She placed herself in the hall under the pretence of doing the flowers. The prosecution say that it was a pretence. The defence say that she was genuinely doing so. You will have to decide which of those two statements is more nearly the truth and the only guidance which I can give you is to remind you of what she herself said when she was being cross-examined. Let me read it to you.

"'You were arranging the flowers in the hall?'

"'In the hall and elsewhere.'

"'Elsewhere?'

"'Yes. In the drawing-room.'

"'What flowers did you put in the drawing-room?'

"'I don't remember. It is some time ago now.'

"'But you do know what you put in the hall.'

"'There were red roses in the hall.'

"'We will come back to them later. Looking after the flowers was part of your usual duties?'

"'In a supervisory capacity.'

"'What do you mean by that?'

"'That I did not always do them myself but I saw that they were properly done.'

"'I see. But you did them occasionally yourself?'

"'Yes.'

"'Who did them normally, by the way?'

"You will remember," Mr. Justice Smith looked up from his reading, and looked at the jury, "that the witness hesitated for a considerable time before she answered that question. Eventually her reply was, 'The housemaid, I think'.

"'You only think? But if you did not approve of the way in which they were done, didn't you want to speak about it? And for that you must have known to whom you had to speak?'

"'If they were wrong, I put them right myself. I don't like criticizing my juniors. It seems, somehow, impertinent.'

"'But this would only be advising. At the most it would be constructive criticism. Would it surprise you to know that Raikes generally looked after them?'

"'It would. It isn't a man's work.'

"On that you will remember that counsel for the Crown intimated that he would recall Raikes to say that he did in fact do that part of the household work, and no doubt you will also remember that the accused admitted that she could not recollect when she had last touched any flower vase at Scotney End Hall, and to the suggestion that she had never done such a thing at all before, she contented herself by replying that she thought she had.

"The prosecution's suggestion therefore is that her desire to arrange the roses on that day was a mere pretence, and all the defence say in answer to this is simply that because she did not habitually undertake that household duty, there is no reason why she should not have done so on that day, and that the delay caused by Mr. Yockleton being with Mr. Cargate, provided a reason, in that she wanted a means of passing the time. It will be for you to decide which of those views is most probable.

"But to continue. The next point concerns the type of roses. The accused in her original statement said that she left the hall to get one more rose from the bed on the lawn outside the library window. She said that it took a little searching as she had picked some from there already and she did not want to spoil the appearance of the bed. The prosecution state that that is entirely untrue and that she invented this explanation to account for her having been out of the hall for a short period during which she was under the impression that Raikes had passed through the hall and gone out through the door leading to the servants' quarters. In fact, Raikes was still in the dining-room, and the movement of the door was not caused by his going out through it but by Mrs. Perriman putting her head in at the door and calling to him.

"There was therefore, so far as Raikes was concerned, no need for her to have accounted for her absence. There might have been in connection with Mrs. Perriman's momentary glance in, but you will remember that though she said in her examination in chief that she believed that the hall was empty when she called Raikes, she admitted in cross-examination that the door impeded her view, and that she did not look carefully.

"But whether Joan Knox Forster was known to have been away for a minute or two during that period, is immaterial, because her own original statement is that she was, and she thought it necessary to explain what she was doing, and the strongest point in the prosecution's case is that, at any rate according to them, that explanation is untrue.

"They claim to prove it as follows. The roses which actually were in the bowl in the hall were Étoile d'Hollande. Raikes, with no knowledge that it was important, called the attention of Inspector Fenby to this fact. It is suggested by the defence—I will return to this point later—that you must not credit the evidence of Raikes, and that possibly he even tampered with the roses, but the first statement as to the contents of that bowl was given quite casually and before any real idea was in anybody's mind, so far as is known, that the identity of the roses was of the slightest importance.

"Inspector Fenby has told you that when Raikes called his attention to the roses, he looked at them. The Inspector does not happen to be interested in gardening, and he does not pretend to know the names of the various types of roses, but he has had his powers of observation trained, and he says that he saw a very dark crimson rose with a great number of petals. Raikes too called his attention to their scent, and he agrees that it was very powerful.

"Now this description would be perfectly accurate with the variety of rose mentioned by Raikes, namely Étoile d'Hollande. But it would be quite inaccurate of the rose growing outside the window of the library. That was called K. of K. and is a loose-petalled rose, only semi-double, with its yellow centre showing directly it is at all fully blown. Moreover, K. of K. is a much brighter red than is Étoile d'Hollande, so that, so the prosecution say, if one of the former had been placed inadvertently amongst the latter, it would have been readily observed.

"And it was not observed.

"Indeed Inspector Fenby went further. He said that he was certain that there was only one kind of rose in the bowl.

"Now Inspector Fenby looked at that bowl twice. The first time we have already mentioned. The second time was when the accused herself asked his leave to throw the flowers away. That occurred on the Saturday evening, and this time he looked at them for a long while because he began to think that there was something wrong about them, though at the moment he could not think what it was. Therefore he is prepared to swear that every one of the flowers in the vase was of the darker variety. Moreover, on this occasion, Mr. Ley was also with him and, though he is not so confident as Inspector Fenby, he also has a very strong impression that there was no K. of K. rose in that bowl.

"But that is not all. You will remember that Knox Forster in her first statement said that it took her some time to select a rose as some had been picked by her already. Now it happened that Mr. Ley in the course of quite casual conversation with Hardy the gardener at Scotney End Hall, made a reference to a 'very fine second bloom'. It was, from a horticultural point of view, a gross error, because at the time it was July, and the second bloom does not occur until September, but it elicited a remark from Hardy to Inspector Fenby directly Mr. Ley was out of earshot. Hardy was rather contemptuous about Mr. Ley and his second bloom, I am afraid" (Mr. Justice Smith allowed himself a smile), "and he went on to say, 'not one of these has been picked this year'. It was that conversation that remained in Inspector Fenby's mind, and caused him to begin to take an active interest in the roses.

"So you see then that the prosecution say that they have convicted the accused in two lies, and that she had neither during that important minute and a half on Thursday, July 12th, nor before, picked a rose from that particular bed, and that in addition no rose from that bed was in the bowl in the hall. Their witnesses to this were Inspector Fenby, Mr. Ley and Raikes, and you have heard what they have said.

"The prosecution allege therefore that Knox Forster is proved to be untruthful, and they suggest that she must have a reason for this fabrication. They say that during that minute and a half she went, not into the garden, but into the library, and that she took out of the bottle a little of that poison and put it into a flower bowl of which she had possessed herself, and that then she slipped quickly into the drawing-room and that there she proceeded to grind down the crystals.

"In support of this story, which counsel for the Crown had necessarily to admit was to some extent an hypothesis, it is pointed out that she originally neglected to mention that she had ever been into the drawing-room at all and that in fact we should never have known that she had gone there unless Raikes had seen her and told us. She now says that she recollects that she did look in for a few seconds and peered at a bowl there which was scratched, but she had forgotten all about it as a trivial detail. You will have to decide whether to accept that explanation.

"But there is no doubt but that the bowl was scratched. The defence say it was done previously and that the accused was actually examining it, but they offer no explanation as to how that fact came to her notice, for I think that it will not be denied that those scratches would not be visible to a casual inspection from a distance. Moreover how was that damage done? The prosecution say that force had to be used to grind down the crystals and they commented sarcastically on the improbability of it being done by the stalk of a rose or any other flower. The defence content themselves with saying that they do not know how those marks were made and they aver, quite truthfully, that they are under no necessity to put up an alternative theory.

"That then briefly is the Crown's submission as to how the poison was obtained and prepared. I have dealt with the defence's suggestions as to the bowl, but I have not yet dealt fully with what they say as to the roses.

"They do not say very much, but briefly they say that Miss Knox Forster made a slip when she originally said that she picked the roses from the front of the house, that actually it was at the back, but that she forgot this, and that such a mistake was a very easy one to make. They then go on to say that she did actually pick one rose at the time she said that she did, but the very fact that its colour was brighter caused it to look odd and that someone must have removed it. No one has been found who says that he or she did so.

"Next then the deceased returned to his library, and there is no dispute as to what happened until the gong rang for lunch. Now in her original statement Knox Forster volunteered the information that she was rather angry with the deceased because on that occasion he did not wash his hands. According to her, he said that he was hungry and they both went straight in to lunch.

"On the other hand Raikes to begin with volunteered the

information that he gave them a few minutes to wash and settle down and that this took about the ordinary time. At first sight there is no serious discrepancy between these two assertions because Raikes might have given time for them to do what in fact, though without his knowledge, they did not do. But you must remember that, for the somewhat strange reasons which he has given to you, Raikes was anxious to be certain that his master was safely seated inside the dining-room and he took simple precautions to watch the progress of events.

"Scotney End Hall is an L-shaped house, and the kitchen premises run away from the front door. If you imagine that door to be towards the left centre of the bottom stroke, the kitchen, pantry and so forth would be at the top of the downward line, so that one side would have looked out on to the lawn at the side of the house if there had been any windows on that side, and the other on the back yard. Towards the right-hand end of the bottom stroke of the L and at the back was a small lavatory with hot and cold water laid on. The pipe from this ran into a drain which was open at the ground level. Consequently water from this basin could be seen as it ran out of the pipe into the drain if anyone chose to look out of the windows of the kitchen or the pantry.

"And Raikes did choose to look, because it was the deceased's habit to wash before lunch and Raikes wanted to know when he had done so, in order to be able to estimate the progress of events.

"Therefore he looked and, as he has sworn to you, he based the timing of his actions on the fact that he saw water running out of the pipe into the drain. Moreover he has said that it was unusual for Miss Knox Forster to use that wash-hand basin. She, however, maintains that he was mistaken, and that both she and Cargate went straight in to lunch. It will be for you to decide which of those statements is true.

"And it is not unimportant. Because it is unlikely, though not impossible, that either of them is making a genuine error. It is more probable that one or other of them is lying deliberately. If Raikes is lying, then it may be, as the defence say, in order to throw suspicion on the accused and possibly away from himself, but if you believe that it is Miss Knox Forster who is telling a deliberate untruth, then you will have to admit that it is possible that she occupied those few moments in mixing up the powder, into which she had already turned the crystals, with the snuff. I must point out to you, what indeed is obvious and freely admitted by the Crown, that there is no proof that she did so, only that she had an opportunity to do so and that, if she is lying, it provides an object for that prevarication.

"So much for that point. We now have to turn to the car.

"It is common ground that something went wrong with the car on that afternoon and that although it was possible, though with difficulty, to convey the witness Macpherson from and to Larkingfield station, by the Friday morning it was out of action, despite the efforts of Miss Knox Forster on Thursday afternoon to put it right. Nor is it denied that Mr. Ley found out on the Saturday afternoon that, in his words, a bit of cotton waste had got drawn up into the exhaust and jammed in it. Mr. Ley removed it and the car was in order again.

"It was perhaps a pity that Mr. Ley was so competent. It would have been interesting to have seen that piece of cotton waste and to have examined it, but unfortunately Mr. Ley destroyed it.

"Nevertheless when Inspector Fenby heard this from Mr.

Ley himself, it occurred to him, as it must have occurred to every one of us, that pieces of cotton waste do not get sucked automatically up the exhausts of cars, and he eventually made an examination which he well might have made before."

"And that," thought Fenby, listening carefully to Sir Trefusis's remarks, "is one in the eye for me because I have an uneasy feeling that I ought to have thought of it earlier. All the same the car was the one thing which was *not* in any way connected with the crime. Moreover I wonder whether it did immediately occur to everyone that the exhaust could not get choked accidentally, or whether even it is quite certainly true?"

"When, however, the Inspector did at length examine the car," Mr. Justice Smith's voice continued quite dispassionately, "an event which did not occur until the following Monday—he found traces, albeit very faint traces, of plaster of Paris in the exhaust, and it is suggested to you that that could not have come there naturally. At first sight it seems difficult to see, even if the car was intentionally put out of action, what that had to do with Cargate's death.

"It is still not clear, but it is an undoubted fact, that Knox Forster, on hearing that the car had been put right, instantly remarked what a merciful fact it was that Cargate had not died of heart failure whilst driving, as he was in the habit of going fast and might have killed or injured one or more innocent passers-by. You will have to decide whether that was a natural humane remark which any of us might have made, or whether it was an idea so much in her mind, that she took steps to prevent such a tragedy occurring and then, directly it was mentioned, blurted out her fears, being at that time under the impression that Cargate's death had been ascribed to purely natural causes."

"My lord," Vernon got on to his feet, "my client has sworn that she suspected from the first that Inspector Fenby's enquiries were of more than a routine nature, and that she went out of her way to assist him in making those enquiries while he was still keeping up the part of being merely sent by the coroner as a matter of course. By the time that she commented to Mr. Ley on the danger of driving with a weak heart, she was well aware that there was a doubt as to how Mr. Cargate died, although it is my submission that she was still unaware of the actual cause."

For a fraction of a second Mr. Justice Smith looked a trifle disconcerted. Then he went on. "Very well then, the jury will bear that in mind, but in any case I was about to inform them that this was largely a speculation and slightly outside the case of either side. Moreover, I must point out that the car was not examined, other than by Mr. Ley, whose evidence was regrettably vague, until the Monday.

"That then is the story which the prosecution has put before you. The defence tell you that it is vague in its details, hypothetical, and that it does not amount to proof. You will give that point of view careful consideration.

"Nevertheless the defence have to admit that somebody placed potassium cyanide in the deceased's snuffbox between the hours of 9.45 a.m. and 3.30 p.m., or at any rate 5 p.m. on that afternoon, even if they do not concede that that poison was the direct cause of death.

"They have suggested that there were three other people who might have done so; Mr. Yockleton in defence of religion and his parish, Mr. Macpherson in an attempt to protect the stamp trade, and Raikes because he was under notice to leave or perhaps, since we seem fated in this case to be given peculiar and unusual motives, out of horror at the breakdown of his master's manhood. You will remember the strange scene which he described in terms which I, for one, found rather moving.

"What is it, Mr. Vernon? You seem to be about to object to that sentence. The jury will, I am sure, understand that I am not trying to prejudice them in favour of Raikes but merely expressing a personal opinion as to the sentimental effect of one incident not too directly connected with the crime.

"Very well then. To continue. You will notice that the motives of each of these three people is not very strong. Perhaps not so strong as in the case of Knox Forster who, you will remember, did not conceal in the witness box that she had, at the very least, an intense dislike for Mr. Cargate and his opinions.

"But to return to the other three. Counsel for the Crown has already pointed out the difficulties which beset the path of assuming any of those three to be guilty unless we assume a great deal of Raikes's evidence to be untrue. Mr. Blayton has simplified my task by going into the points involved in some detail, and the barest outline will suffice for me to recapitulate them."

The seats of the jury box were getting harder and harder, and it was with relief that Ellis and his fellow jurymen found that Mr. Justice Smith intended to be as good as his word. It did not take him very long to deal with the three other possibles, but it was also abundantly clear that in the opinion of the learned Judge they were barely possible at all. In a short while he swept all three of them aside and turned to another point. "And finally," he said, "we have the position of the snuffbox and the bottle.

"A careful examination of this has been put before you and I shall not detain you long over the matter. As to the snuffbox, you will have observed that Raikes definitely stated that it was by Cargate's left hand, and that Miss Knox Forster said it was by his right hand both at the same time of the morning and that Macpherson said that later in the afternoon it was by the deceased's left-hand side. Quite what the prosecution deduce from this, I am not quite clear. The defence say that it just shows how inaccurate Knox Forster was, that it was a genuine mistake made in good faith, and that she was quite capable of making similar mistakes over, for instance, the roses. You must decide how much, if any, importance is to be attached to that.

"As to the position of the small bottle of poison, it was certainly on the table at 10.45, for here Raikes is confirmed by Mr. Yockleton. At twelve o'clock it was certainly on the window-sill, if you believe Hardy the gardener. Indeed it was there at 11.38 if you think that Raikes is speaking the truth in what he reports that the deceased said. Apparently it did not move in effect afterwards although it might have been picked up and put down again. But just after eleven-thirty, when, according to Miss Knox Forster, she went out to get the rose, if she did go out, it was on the window-sill.

"Was it? The defence say that it was, and Cargate himself put it there. The prosecution say that it was not but that the accused thought that it was and that therefore, when she picked it up, as they say, at about 11.32, she put it down again, not on the table, but on the window-sill. You must remember that in their submission she did not go out into the garden at that time at all and so did not see it through the window.

"Well, members of the jury, I think that that is all I can say that will be of assistance to you. You will now retire and consider your verdict."

Part VI
Verdict

John Ellis led his party into the bleak and dreary room provided for the jury. Somehow it seemed all the more dank because they had to consider what had happened on two or more hot days in July.

All through the case he had been dreading this moment when—as he supposed—he would have to give a lead to the other eleven, for Ellis, though not a vain man, had a definite opinion of his own value, and he thought that if he made up his own mind definitely, he would have little difficulty in getting the others to agree with him.

And the worst of it was that he had come to no decision. He wanted very much to have an interval for quiet reflection as he would have done if it had been a matter connected with the ministry in which he held the rank of principal. There, although he genuinely worked extremely hard, he was not as a rule called upon to give a decision in a hurry. And indeed, to his mind, the system was a wise one. He was sure, for instance, that all his fellow jurymen would have been more capable of giving a correct verdict after a night's sleep. That, perhaps, such a delay would not be welcome to the accused, did not occur to him; it never worried him to keep the public waiting if there was, in his eyes, a good reason, and he saw no reason to alter his practice in this case.

But now, owing to this improper haste, he was undecided, and he dreaded one of his colleagues coming out with a definite statement too soon, because he knew that it was then only too likely that he would take the opposite view out of sheer perverseness. For at all times his nicely poised mind recoiled from any case that was overstated. Indeed all through the trial he had been conscious of a desire to contradict both Blayton and the Judge, simply because they seemed so certain. Vernon, on the other hand, had been so much more reasonable. He had continually taken the line of saying, "Well, of course it might have happened like that. But it might equally have been—" It was a method which appealed to Ellis, but perhaps not to all the rest of the jury.

So it came about that there was a noticeably long silence in the jury room which at last was broken by a seedy looking little man in a black suit with a green tie and a high single collar which hardly opened at all in front. "Method," he said suddenly, "that's what we've got to use. I always say that to my wife when it comes to running our shop. Fish, Pritchett and Hanson. In Market Square. And very good fish too. Pleased to serve any of you." He delved in his pocket for his trade cards.

"I think you are quite right," Ellis answered gravely, trying not to allow his internal merriment at the little man's opportunism to be too apparent. "We must consider the matter methodically."

"And the first thing—leastways the thing that seems to me to come first"—the large farmer seemed rather surprised to find himself talking at all, and even more startled to notice that everyone was listening to him—"is this. Was he poisoned, or did he just die?"

"Does it really matter?" A rather decided young man, probably a bank clerk put in. "He was meant to be killed anyhow."

"It would make the difference between murder and attempted murder, I suppose." Ellis felt that somebody had to answer the question. "And I imagine—in fact I am sure—that the penalties are very different."

"She's only been accused of murder, hasn't she. Does that make a difference? I only just want to know." The fourth juryman was an assistant in a bookshop in the assize town, and had the rest of the jury been aware of it, he went through life saying that he "only just wanted to know".

"We can, if necessary, ask the Judge," Ellis answered. "I am not a lawyer, but I believe we could find her guilty of attempted murder if we liked. But perhaps the question won't arise."

An amused smile came across the face of a superior looking man, who was neither quite a gentleman nor quite a farmer, but who thought that he was undoubtedly both, and did at any rate know that Ellis's remarks, especially as to attempted murder, were wide of the mark. "I was under the impression, Mr. Foreman, that the jury were required to find the facts and that the law was usually left to the Judge. At any rate there is a popular superstition to that effect."

"We don't seem to have been directed about it." Ellis was angry with himself for being so helpless. "I mean about the difference."

"I think we were," a rather stout, retired farmer broke in. "We all heard what the Judge said about even a chap with a bad heart being entitled to have a chance. And for him to

peg out nice and neatly and opportunely like that, just afore
he took the snuff, wouldn't be in the nature of things. No, if
you ask my opinion it's murder all right, and there's no need
to split hairs about it. Judge practically said so."

There was a general murmur of assent in which even the
superior man joined. "And really," thought Ellis, "they're
almost certainly right. I don't think I need make them think
that over again. Very well, then," he said aloud, "that preliminary point is settled."

"That's right," the man in the green tie broke in, "that's
method, that is."

"Then the next point is, I suppose," Ellis began to take
charge, "to see if we agree that anyone can be eliminated.
Shall we start with Macpherson?"

"He's our man," the bank clerk put in suddenly. "You
never can trust these stamp dealers. I had a lovely collection
once—over two thousand and all different—but when I tried
to sell it, do you think I could get anything for it? Not even
half a dollar. Now, if I had wanted to buy it—"

"But is that any reason for suggesting—?"

"Perhaps not, Mr. Foreman. But they're a dishonest lot
anyhow. Mixed perforations indeed! Whatever that may
mean. Mixed morals, I should say too."

"And perhaps rather mixed ideas." The superior man
looked at the ceiling.

"This isn't methodical." The fish merchant was at least
consistent.

"I don't think, you know," Ellis, sighing for the orderliness
of his office, kept his temper admirably, "that we ought to
consider anything that was not given to us as evidence. I
am sure that we all sympathize with you about your stamp
collection, but I thought that when Macpherson gave his
evidence, he seemed to be speaking perfectly truthfully."

"Well, I'm all for finding him guilty." The abortive sale of the stamp collection seemed still to be rankling deeply.

"I don't think we can do that. We can only bring in a verdict of 'guilty' or 'not guilty' in the case of Miss Knox Forster."

"The foreman's right there—"

"What, can't we hang that blasted butler—slimy brute?" The retired farmer seemed genuinely surprised.

"I'm afraid not. I was suggesting that we should first decide whether we could eliminate—leave out—Macpherson. Would you like to consider the points about him first?"

"The Judge did that, didn't he?" The superior man's voice was intolerably urbane. "I propose that we leave out both Macpherson and Yockleton—silly sort of name anyhow."

"I second that." The remark came from a man who had not spoken before, but who acted on the principle that it helped to reach a decision rapidly if every proposition was immediately seconded. In his opinion it brought things to an issue, and curbed unnecessary discussion, and at any committee meeting which he attended he made an invariable practice of seconding everything—occasionally absent-mindedly seconding the opposition to something whose proposal he had already attempted to secure.

But it did not always work in practice as a time-saving device because very often people, quite unnecessarily, seemed prompted to oppose what was put forward. Of course that was all right if the chairman had the sense to take an immediate vote, but so very often he allowed people to express the reasons which led them to hold their views, and that invariably wasted a great deal of time, and, so far as could be found out, never caused anyone to alter his or her opinion. And so in this case it turned out to be. Quite an animated debate began to grow up as to the possibility of Macpherson being guilty. Very often it even had some connection with the evidence that had been given.

Eventually, however, Ellis managed to regain some control over the meeting. "Perhaps it would clear the air if we voted on the matter."

"I second that. Ought to have voted long ago."

"Those in favour of the view that Macpherson did not do it? Ten and myself—eleven. Against?"

The bank clerk shrugged his shoulders. "Very well then—have it your own way. And if we can't hang him anyhow, it doesn't matter."

"Now to turn to the rector—Mr. Yockleton. Can we take a similar vote?"

"I second that."

Ellis looked round, and to his pleasure found that they were unanimous. "Then it comes to this. Either the accused did it, that means we vote 'guilty', or Raikes did it, in which case we vote 'not guilty', or we don't know which of them did it, in which case we again vote 'not guilty'."

"Too many suggestions of 'not guilty' if you ask my opinion. The Judge seemed to have made up his mind quite easily." The superior man again contemplated the ceiling.

"Ah, but you must look at it the way the foreman says— that's method, that is."

"Thank you, Mr. Pritchett."

"Hanson."

"Mr. Hanson, I should say. Now just to start the discussion, I'm going to suggest that she wasn't guilty at all, or at any rate that it isn't proved. It seemed to me that the Judge was a great deal too biased against her. He ought to have stressed the points in her defence more clearly. As it was, I don't think that he was fair. For instance, she was a decent, peaceful sort of woman who could never have brought herself to commit a murder. Why, it even came out that she was a conscientious objector, and couldn't bring herself to take life."

"Not quite that." Mr. Hanson began to contribute to the discussion something more positive than his previous remarks. "Only that she disapproved of war, which we all do, though we may differ in our ideas as to how to stop it. But there wasn't anything to say that she disapproved of taking wasps' nests. And that's what she did, if you ask me. She'd been living under the same roof as Cargate for months, and hating him every minute of it, hating him more and more every day and having to listen to him putting forward opinions which seemed to her to be downright wicked, and behaving to everybody in a way that she couldn't stand. And all the time she had to disguise her feelings until she was ready to burst. And finally she did burst. Or rather he did."

"Isn't that rather an assumption?"

"It's what the Judge thought anyhow, and, if you ask me, it's true. Personally I think she was absolutely right, but I suppose we mustn't take that into consideration."

"I think there can be no doubt, Mr. Foreman" (Ellis found that he intensely disliked being called "Mr. Foreman" by the superior man, but he had to admit that it did bring the discussion back to the point), "that she lied about that rose. And about the scratches on the bowl, if you ask me. And about the time at which they went in to lunch."

"No doubt about the former. I've got both those sorts of roses in my garden, and you can't possibly mistake one for the other." The retired farmer spoke more from experience than from evidence.

"It seems to me that there are two possible answers to that," Ellis replied. "First of all, she is very short-sighted, and anyhow knows less about roses than you do. And secondly Raikes may have deliberately thrown away the one she put in."

"You're being too clever, mister," a hitherto silent juryman broke in. "How would Raikes know whether it mattered or not?"

"He called attention to the type of roses in the bowl. It seems to me that he was trying to bring them to the Inspector's notice."

"But he didn't know she was going to say that."

"Supposing he heard her talking to the Inspector?"

"You bet he couldn't. The police are too fly for that."

"All the same," Ellis found his own opinion weakening, "we ought to be quite sure before we decide. I am sure you all want to consider everything that there is to be said for her."

"The Judge didn't find much to say," the superior man commented. "He knows a lot more about these things than we do. He's had more experience of witnesses trying to lie to him than we have, and he saw through her all right. Besides no one else could have done it. We all agree—at least practically we all agree—that it could not have been anyone but her or Raikes, and it couldn't have been Raikes because he's got a cast-iron alibi all the time unless you're going to say what nobody has so far, that the cook was in it with him. There isn't a scrap of evidence to support it, whereas with the other woman, there's the roses, there's the bowl, there's the washing, and there's the car. I attach rather a lot of importance myself to the car. It just fits in with her type. No war, no; but a murder, yes. A murder, yes; but an accident, no. Don't like those sort of people. Much better hanged."

"Do you know, somehow I don't feel that that's quite fair. For that matter, I didn't feel that the Judge was entirely impartial."

"Really if you are going to say things against the Judge! I mean, you can't do that!"

"I'm not. Only that this particular Judge had made up his mind too definitely."

"Well, he ought to give us a lead, oughtn't he? That's method, isn't it?"

"It may be, but it is also method that we consider all the evidence, and only the evidence." Ellis felt himself compelled to go on fighting, even though he was beginning to think that it was a losing battle and that he himself was not so certain.

From the far end of the room came a little whispering amongst the more silent members of the jury. "We five here, Mr. Foreman, have made up our minds. We say 'guilty'."

Ellis looked round and listened to a chorus of "agreed". Even the farmer who had wanted to hang Raikes, seemed to have changed his mind. For a full minute he hesitated, then he said: "No, we can't have a verdict unless it is unanimous, and I can't square it with my conscience to fall in line with you unless not only I but you have reviewed all the evidence. I do put it to you that it is our duty to do so and that we can't avoid it."

"I must say, Mr. Foreman, that I find your conscience somewhat tiresome."

"I second that."

"But there's method in it."

"I'm sorry, but I insist. If you are all still of the same mind, then it may be another matter, but otherwise it almost seems as if we were not taking an intelligent interest in it."

"Well, really." There was a general movement which showed that Ellis had gone too far. Nevertheless, up to a point, he won his case. The jury consented rather more systematically than might have been expected, but still rather discursively, to consider the case. It took them over two hours and they were not by the end at all pleased with each other.

● ● ● ● ●

The Clerk of Assize rose and put the usual question. "Members of the jury, are you agreed upon your verdict?"

"We are."

"Do you find the prisoner at the bar" (he gave the name in full) "guilty or not guilty?"

Ellis intimated in one word that he had been unable to shake his fellow jurors' original opinion.

The Clerk of Assize turned to the accused.

Part VII
Conclusion

In the quiet of a small house in Dorset in the valley of the Frome, in which he was hoping to enjoy many placid, happy days fishing, Sir Trefusis Smith read his *Times* contentedly. He had thought that he could rely on the Court of Criminal Appeal, and now he saw that he had been right.

It had always been his intention to retire directly after the trial of Joan Knox Forster, and he had carried it into immediate execution. And really, though with the report of the appeal in front of them many people might not have thought so, it had been rather an heroic ending. For he had never had the slightest doubt as to the guilt of the accused. Even his combative reactions to Anstruther Blayton's discursive methods—competent though they had been—had not allowed him to take any other view. Nor, in his opinion, could any jury have come to any other conclusion than that which had been reached by Ellis and his colleagues, for all Vernon's efforts could not cover up the fact that his client was far too honest and had practically given herself away in the box.

All through, that had been the trouble. It seemed an odd thing to think about a woman who had committed a murder, and other people might not agree with him, but he had a very definite respect, almost amounting to admiration, for her. For one thing, he thoroughly agreed with her opinion of Cargate's character, which perforce had not been spared by either side at the trial. To Sir Trefusis, a picture of Cargate had gradually been presented in which he appeared to be, if possible, even worse than he had been in life.

And, with that in his mind, the tall, clumsy woman had seemed so essentially honest. He had liked her. He even, though he did not agree with them, respected her political ideas, and finally he came to the conclusion that, guilty though she was, it would be a pity if she were to be hanged.

It had been rather a shock to him to reach that point, and at first he had been inclined to push it aside as pure senility, mixed with the sentiment arising from the knowledge that it was his own last case. He had never been anything other than a realist in his life before. In fact the very idea that English criminal law should be based on sentiment and not justice was absolutely abhorrent to him. Once admit that, except in self-defence, killing could ever be justified, and there would, in his opinion, be an end of all safety and sanity in the country. And that he, who had been regarded as something of a hanging Judge, should allow such a doctrine to creep in, was an impossible and intolerable idea.

No. All through the trial he had placed before himself firmly the objective that that must not happen; even a verdict of "not guilty" he had regarded as extremely undesirable, because, to his mind, it would be so obviously contrary to the facts, that it would be generally considered to be based on inclination, and once such a precedent crept in, there was no knowing where it would end.

Nevertheless as he had listened to Blayton's fair but remorseless representations, he had wished more and more strongly to preserve both the principle on which the law rested, and the life of the accused. It had seemed hard at first, but gradually a way had become clear to him. It involved some sacrifice of his own reputation, but he had never cared much for that. If his conscience acquitted him, the rest of the world might go hang.

It had been a temptation to take the point offered by Vernon, and withdraw the case from the jury on the ground that Cargate had not been proved ever to have died of poison at all, but his judicial sense had made it quite impossible for him to do so. He simply could not bring himself to say that there was no evidence on which the jury might find that the poison had in fact been taken. Indeed the point seemed to him to be exactly the opposite way round. He had no doubt whatever that Cargate had been murdered.

So finally he had decided to take up the line that he did, and it had been perfectly and entirely successful. Indeed he had always thought that it would be, although for about half an hour he wondered whether he had overdone it. It was possible, he knew, to put things too plainly to a jury, and so end by finding them asserting their independence by bringing in a contrary verdict. If he was any judge of character, the foreman of that particular jury had been just such a type of man.

However, justice had been vindicated by the verdict, and now humanity had triumphed in the Court of Criminal Appeal. He had succeeded in obtaining both his objectives. There would be no execution.

With a contented smile, he skimmed through the column. "Brought out every point against the accused... did not mention those which might have been in her favour... would instance in particular that it was not mentioned that the accused was shortsighted... knew nothing of botany or gardening… conceivably pardonable errors…" Yes, Vernon had picked up neatly most of the points on which Sir Trefusis had relied for his ultimate result. Indeed he had added a few which, to Sir Trefusis's mind were less good. He did not think that it was quite fair to say that he had minimized the possibility of the other three being the criminal. Personally he thought that he had put that quite fairly, but it was equally proper for Vernon to suggest that he had not. He had to remind himself rather sharply that it was irrational for him to be irritated by that.

Ah! But here at last was the point on which he had mainly relied. He thought that he had seen Vernon quickly conceal a smile of approaching triumph when he left that out, and here it was. He nodded with satisfaction. Yes, it was perfectly true. He had never told the jury that they must be satisfied beyond reasonable doubt, and that if they were not, that it was their duty… The phrases had come so naturally to him, that it had been quite hard to keep them back.

But he had not said them, and by that negation, coupled with the general adverse trend of his summing-up, he had made, he had always thought, practically certain that the Court of Criminal Appeal would be bound to quash the verdict. And now he saw that they had done so. It almost made him laugh to see the careful way in which they had attempted to spare his feelings. Their intentions were as excellent as he felt his own to have been. But the great thing was that they had done it. He was glad, thoroughly glad of the final result of the trial in connection with the murder of Launcelot Henry Cuthbert Cargate.

Dear Reader,

We want to tell you about Richard Hull, a writer with whom you may or may not be familiar. Here is a chance to find out more!

Richard Hull wrote 15 novels. He worked as an accountant in private practice and, during the Second World War, he also worked for the Admiralty in this capacity.

Arguably Hull's most well-known novel was *The Murder of My Aunt*, originally published in 1934. This was Hull's first novel and its success encouraged and convinced Hull to become a full-time writer. His trademarks throughout many of his novels are his humour and his unexpected, intriguing endings. He includes unreliable narrators in his work, and writes from the different perspectives of victims and criminals alike.

Richard Hull was a member of the Detection Club, and even assisted Agatha Christie with her duties as President.

If you liked this story, why don't you sign up to the Crime Classics newsletter where you can discover more about Richard Hull, more about Golden Age crime and beloved greats of the Golden Age. On signing you will receive exclusive material, information and news. It takes less than a minute to sign up. You can get your first newsletter by signing up on the website www.crimeclassics.co.uk

So do join the community!

—Richard Hull literary Estate

To see more Poisoned Pen Press titles:

Visit our website:
poisonedpenpress.com
Request a digital catalog:
info@poisonedpenpress.com